The Legacy

By Kyle Berkley

Published By:
Bold Print Publishing

Bold Print Publishing • 5334 Wyndholme Circle Baltimore MD 21229

Ordering Information:
Quantity sales. Special discounts are available on quantity purchases by corporations, associations, and others. For details, contact the publisher at the address above.

Orders by U.S. trade bookstores and wholesalers.
Please contact info@KyleSBerkley.com

Book Cover Artwork by: Stacie Doi
Edited by: Karen Rodgers

ISBN: 979-8-9877806-1-9
Copyright © 2023 Kyle S. Berkley
All rights reserved.

Dedication

This book is dedicated to my father, Samuel Berkley. My Uncle Elisha Garland, my cousin Kenneth Bowman, my best friend Chris Burton, my friends Kevin Brown, Antonio Washington a.k.a. Tony Bones and so many other brothers and sisters we have lost over the years.

Acknowledgments

Before I start, I would like to state this acknowledgment section will be a lot shorter than *The Wake's*, not because nothing changed, but because there were a lot of names. I first want to give all thanks to my creator, all the great things I have accomplished would not have happened without Him. A kid from West Port, Baltimore City that has published books, and college graduated, with a Ph.D.! WOW! I have to give thanks to my loving and supportive wife, and my three beautiful daughters, Savannah, Sage, and Shiloh. I wish I could put hearts by all of their names. They're my whole world. I also have to thank my parents for all they have poured into me to become the man I am today. Thanks also to my sisters Kyrissa, Kim, Toi, Sharay and Brenda and my brothers Lamont, Andre, Anthony, Angelo, Charles, John Mark, and Reggie. I would like to give thanks to Odessa Rose, Ashley Logan Graham and Cheryl Barton . I would like to give special thanks to my family and friends that have helped me throughout my life. I genuinely love you all. I can't move past this section without giving thanks to the lawyers and members of the LGBTQ community that gave me so much input into certain chapters of this story. I also want to thank each and every person that purchased *The Wake* and *The Void*. It meant so much to be supported and promoted the way I have been over the years.

Table of Contents

Prologue

Fair warning, those of you who have not yet read my two previous books, The Wake and The Void, from this sentence forward, this book contains many spoilers. I urge you to stop here and consider purchasing those books first to get the full story.

Tiffany Gibbons, a beautiful 35-year-old African American woman and her best friend Sasha Green were displaced from their apartment building, thanks to a community redevelopment effort led by Titan Industries. Titan Industries is owned by twin adult siblings, Chandler and Chanel Titan, along with married couple Sedrick and Erica Little. Tiffany's grandmother, community leader Florence Simms, and her former pastor, Donald Avery fought against the efforts of Titan Industries until their untimely deaths.

During the same time, Tiffany's youngest daughter, Kenya, and her baby's father, Keyon, were murdered in a hit-and-run car accident.Tiffany's best friend, Sasha experienced the death of her high-school-age son, Tyrone Clinton at the hands of the Baltimore City Police during a botched robbery. It was later learned that Tyrone did not want to take part in the armed robbery, but was bullied into participating. Unfortunately, when he attempted to give himself up to the responding police, he was murdered.

Tyrone Clinton was a star football player for a local high school, who was coached by local police officer, Edward Carter. Edward Carter and Tyrone made a deal that if he improved his grades, Tyrone could use the coach's BMW for the prom. Tyrone had hoped to take his longtime crush, Tina Simms, to the prom. Following the murder of an unarmed high school student, Kennard Lyles-Bey, Edward Carter went to the local hospital to speak to Mr. Lyles-Bey's parents, against Police Commissioner Alex Tillman's orders. Edward Carter was killed by what were assumed to be rioters, following an exchange of gunfire. Alex Tillman murdered the two presumed rioters.

Sadly, Tiffany's aunt, Gina Simms remained deeply entrenched in her drug addiction for several years. During that time she befriended a young transwoman named Silk, born Simon Little, a former radio personality who was fired for sleeping with the radio station owner's husband during a highly publicized function. Silk's parents, Erica and Sedrick Little were resentful of Silk and being forced to accept her sexual identity. This became the catalyst for the murder of Silk at the hands of Tiffany's father.

Sedrick and Erica attempted to have a private funeral for Silk at the Allen Bradley Funeral Home during the same time that Florence Simms', Donald Avery's, Edward Carter's, Tyrone Clinton's, and Kenya Gibbons' services were held. Gina Simms revealed Silk's birth name, Simon Little, and alerted Anna Cartright, the local news media personality covering the service for Tyrone Clinton. The City of Baltimore paused the community reconstruction project due to the controversy.

A year after the funeral services, Tiffany and the local community leader turned-impromptu-pastor, Hakeem Andrews began dating. Tiffany moved into the home her grandmother left her, along with her four remaining children. Tiffany's best friend Sasha began living with her but developed a drinking habit to cope with the grief of her deceased son, Tyrone Clinton.

Hakeem has attempted to overcome the challenges in the Ridgely Square community using advocacy to stop Titan Industries in their new search for community redevelopment. Hakeem tried to partner with his estranged brother Jamar, leader of a local mosque. But there were too many differences in their belief systems; for instance, Jamar is of the opinion that the best way for Ridgely Square to thrive is to alienate itself from the rest of Baltimore City and become sovereign. He also alleges that the community should have its own schools, banks, and police department.

Hakeem disagrees with Jamar's assertions, and the two constantly butt heads on these viewpoints. It soon becomes clear that Jamar's previous criminal past has deep unresolved roots tied to Hakeem. Hakeem never went to prison unlike his brother Jamar. In addition to Jamar's incarnation, he was alienated by the family and the family's church. Jamar understood Tiffany's growing concerns about the worsening conditions in her neighborhood, so he provided her with a gun for protection from the local gang known as the Alphas and the rogue police unit known as the Narcotics and Firearms Taskforce.

Finally taking her sobriety seriously, Tiffany's aunt, Gina Simms, attempted to bond with Tiffany and they attended a grief and loss group gathering at the Allen Bradley Funeral Home. Gina also participated in a documentary about police corruption in the Baltimore City communities, specifically Ridgely Square, where she highlighted the actions of a rogue unit of officers called the Narcotics and Firearms Taskforce, also known as NAFA. NAFA has been working with a local gang called the Alphas, raiding the homes of revival gang members, known as the Cabal, taking narcotics and selling them in order to receive cash or gift card payments.

The leader of NAFA, Marshawn Bell, saved the extorted money with the goal of paying for his terminally ill mother's medical treatment at an experimental lab in Virginia. Prior to achieving his goal of paying for her treatment, Marshawn was arrested, thanks to Gina's involvement in the documentary. Marshawn admitted to his illegal actions while expressing his concern about his mother's meager teacher's salary and the fact that medicare insurance did not provide her a competitive chance to thrive.

Marshawn also admitted he put a hit out on Edward Carter because he believed Alex Tillman used Edward Carter to spy on Marshawn's criminal behavior. He also used Jada Carr to get his case thrown out by agreeing to be a witness in a federal trial against the Alphas. Upon Marshawn's release from jail, he attempted to kidnap Sasha Green to assist with medicating his mother until they could reach the treatment center in Virginia, but Sasha was too intoxicated. Marshawn replaced Sasha withTiffany with the goal that Tiffany would keep his mother stable until she reached the medical research center in Newport News, Virginia. Marshawn provided Tiffany with millions of dollars in gift cards for the damage he caused her and the Gibbons family. Upon arrival at the treatment center, Marshawn Bell was murdered by commissioner Alex Tillman.

After Tiffany's return to Baltimore, Sasha agreed to go into substance abuse treatment, and move into Gina's home. After having a heart to heart talk with Sasha, Tiffany finally felt more comfortable talking to her children about the grief and trauma they endured throughout the last year. Gina was placed in witness protection for her upcoming court testimony against the Alphas and NAFA. While going into the basement, a place where Tiffany frequently heard the voices of her grandmother Florence, her daughter Kenya, her cousin Tina and negative words from her father, Daryl Gibbons, Tiffany learned that someone broke into the back door of her home. Tiffany discovered her father, who had repeatedly molested her, and her cousin Tina in the past had broken into her home, with the children right upstairs. Tiffany used the handgun that Jamar had given her weeks before to take the life of her father.

Now the Tiffany Gibbons' saga continues. Welcome to The Legacy. Welcome back to Ridgely Square.

Chapter 1

It's a beautiful spring day in Baltimore City. Outside the sun is shining with a few clouds. Several people in the Ridgely Square Community are walking by my storefront restaurant and fresh food market, which I recently opened. This is great news because the location of my restaurant is in the Old Ridgley Market Place, a large defunct outdoor mall that takes up 3 residential blocks. Almost all of the buildings have been closed and condemned for at least 25 years. Inside the restaurant, I'm sitting at a table with several cameras, a recording crew, and Anna Cartwright. A former Tennessee State's Attorney turned TV personality, after being disgracefully removed from office. Several years ago, Anna and a few judges, took bribes from detention centers in Tennessee to push for heavy convictions, and she purposely hid evidence that impacted several verdicts. Anna would later move to Maryland, work on a nighttime political talk show, then gain a job as a correspondent on Nubian Media, a local TV, radio, and app network. Anna interviewed my aunt Gina for a documentary two years ago. Today, she's interviewing me with the goal of highlighting some positive things happening in the Ridgely Square Community.

"Tiffany, a year ago you graduated college with a degree in social work and decided to open this restaurant,

Legacy of Florence. Can you tell me why, and who Florence was?" Anna asks, sitting across from me with a big bleached blonde hairstyle. Dressed in a navy blue pantsuit and white heels, Anna attempts to make her face look warm and pleasant, but it comes off very disingenuous. I've dealt with Anna in the past, thanks to my aunt Gina, and a whole messy situation she put me through two years ago. I feel somewhat nervous because of all the cameras surrounding me, but at the same time, I feel comfortable because I am sitting in my restaurant.

"Legacy of Florence was named after my grandmother, Florence Simms, who was a community leader, an evangelist at the New Hope Greater Love Church, a teacher for a period of time, and a cook. My grandmother, Florence, turned the church's kitchen into a carryout and fed this community for decades but never officially opened her own restaurant. She also worked with Pastor Donald Avery, the pastor of New Hope Greater Love Church," I answer as Anna leans forward in her chair.

She places her right hand's thumb and index finger on the opposite sides of her chin, slowly rubbing her jawline. "Can you tell the audience a little about Pastor Donald Avery?" she asks while making strong eye contact.

"Pastor Avery's father was from a small town in Virginia and fought in World War II. When he came back home from the war, a pair of white men launched several racial slurs towards him as he walked from the bus station to his family's farm. The men attacked Pastor Avery's father, and he killed them with his bare hands. Pastor Avery was a young boy when he and his parents fled to Baltimore, Maryland a day or two later when the Ku Klux Klan began looking for him. Pastor Avery worked at a paint factory and a steel mill for several years but faced a lot of issues, thanks to Jim Crow laws and redlining in the city," I answer as Anna changes her posture, moving to a complete upright position.

"Can you tell our listeners about the redlining problems Baltimore faced?" Anna asks as a person standing behind a large light on a pole for the camera made a circular motion with her finger.

"The redlining problem, from what I know, was based on a practice to discriminate against African Americans. In Baltimore City, there were a lot of people making decent middle-class wages, well enough to move into nice neighborhoods. The redlining practices stopped them and forced many African Americans into less than desirable neighborhoods, and prevented many African Americans from getting loans. Pastor Avery and his family endured that, which led them to Ridgely Square. A place that my great-great-grandfather called home and built the home my children and I live in today."

"Tell me a little bit about Ridgely Square, that's where we are today. Your restaurant, in what should be a historic district," Anna encourages, leaning back into her chair.

"Ridgely Square was a middle-class neighborhood that many African Americans found themselves in, in Baltimore City, thanks to redlining. Over the years plenty of high rise buildings and subsidized apartment units, what many call projects, were built on the Ridgely Homes part of Ridgely Square," I answer.

"Explain how Ridgely Square is divided."

"The east side of Ridgely Square is where we are now, The Old Market Place. The west side of Ridgely Square has the Ridgely Homes, which includes several residential neighborhoods, some apartment buildings, and another community called Duke Hill, but the people there do not like being associated with Ridgely Square. The south side of Ridgely Square is the Arts District, which has an art school, a few bars, a couple of inns, diners, restaurants, and several residential homes. The north side of Ridgely Square is what many call the school side. You have several houses in that area, subsidized apartments, a recreation center, and a lot of places being demolished due to a reconstruction project headed by Titan Industries."

"Titan Industries is a company that your grandmother, Florence Simms, and Pastor Avery fought against for a while, am I correct?" Anna Cartwright asks as the person standing behind the bright light nods her head at me.

"Yes. My grandmother and Pastor Avery were against Titan Industries and their plan to gentrify Ridgely Square. Ridgely Square became a black Wallstreet from the 1950s until the last decade. The closing down of the steel mills and several factories created many challenges for the homeowners, including the increase in crime. Yet, my grandmother and Pastor Avery believed that Ridgely Square could turn around if given the right help. Titan Industries, currently led by Erica Little, believes that they can purchase the properties here, demolish them, build something else and make it so the people here cannot afford to move back. They have lobbied with Councilman Dawson to obtain permits with the goal of destroying everything in this district, including our schools. The same schools that my children go to. They destroyed the high-rise apartment building my children and I lived in. If it wasn't for my grandmother willing me the house when she died, my children would have been displaced."

"That's very interesting and heartbreaking stuff, Ms. Gibbons. Since Pastor Avery and Florence Simms have died, how do you plan on continuing their legacy?" Anna asks as I lean back in the chair. The nervousness I may have had went completely out the window. Maybe because I am confident, and maybe because I'm hallucinating and seeing a glimpse of my grandmother behind the lady standing next to the light.

"Well, first I completed college a year ago. Fulfilling a promise I made to my grandmother a few years earlier. Secondly, I opened this restaurant and market. In this restaurant, we cook meals from our family's cookbook. We also sell fresh fruit, vegetables, and meats from local farmers. The goal is to combat the food desert problem the city has had over recent years. We also provide education classes on how to prepare healthy meals and I hire people from this community. My fiancé, Dr. Hakeem Andrews, is the current pastor at the New Hope Greater Love Church. He, his brother Jamar, Allen Bradley, the owner and director of the Allen Bradley Funeral Home, Ms. Clair of Nubian Media, and myself started a bank called the 10th Bank. The idea of the 10th Bank is based loosely on W.E.B. DuBois's idea of the talented 10th but with a twist. The 10th Bank is a black-owned banking institution that not only services its participants like most banks, but it also invests in several black-owned companies, such as clothing companies, music companies, schools, stores, and they even provide scholarships."

"I'm confused," Anna says with a puzzled look on her face.

"Imagine you have 100 people. Then you separate the group into 10s. The first group of 10 may want to open a funeral home, the second group may want to open a shoe store, the third group may want to open a supermarket, the fourth group may want to open a drug store. A fifth group may want to open a food carryout. Out of the first group of 10, 1 person receives a loan and becomes successful, the other 9 people in that group learn the skills to become successful while the recipient pays his loan, the other 9 will eventually receive their chance to receive a loan. Same as the 10 people that want to open a supermarket or drug store. The places are also opened in black communities and the people that receive the loans will have to live in the black communities. That is how we circulate the wealth in our community. By following this model we create equity in Ridgely Square and we stop Titan from taking over because we have the means and assets. We also make sure that people do not lose their homes from defaulting on loans or not paying their taxes."

"I'm looking forward to learning more about this program. Now let's shift gears a little bit. It has been two years since the incident with your aunt Gina and the Narcotics and Firearms Task Force. How have you been processing everything?" Anna asks as I notice a brown skinned slim man smiling and standing next to her. It is an illusion of a person I watched get murdered in front of me.

"Where should I start? NAFA, or as you stated the Narcotics and Firearms Task Force, was a group of detectives and police officers led by Marshawn Bell, that abused power and worked with a gang called the Alphas. Together NAFA and the Alphas terrorized Ridgely Square. My aunt Gina, who is now in witness protection, helped provide information to law enforcement to use to take down NAFA and several members of the Alphas. Marshawn Bell kidnapped me in front of my home intending to use his extortion and drug money to get his mother into a cancer treatment facility. Bell was later murdered by our former police commissioner, Alex Tillman, that was watching Bell since his case was dropped at the state level," I answer. I notice a grin on the face of the person standing next to Anna Cartwright and could see it was another hallucination of Marshawn Bell. I have experienced several of these since his murder. Sometimes he will talk to me. Sometimes he will playfully interact with people I speak to. I know that it's not really him, but when he speaks he can be very convincing with his statements.

"What do you know about the ongoing investigation with the Alphas and NAFA?" Anna asks as I try to look away from Bell, who is making funny faces and dancing.

"Bell took a deal with the FBI and the State's Attorney, Jada Austin, intending to identify members of the Alphas involved in the sex trafficking ring. Aunt Gina gave me two USB flash drives that I provided to the FBI that had information on them related to the case. I had no idea what was on the drives. Soon as I located the information, I gave it to an agent. I have nothing to do with the ongoing investigation. I just want to raise my four children and eventually plan my wedding," I answer as I notice a change in Anna's facial expression. A stern, intimidating look falls upon her face as I notice a deep silence in the room.

"While we are all happy about your engagement, your restaurant, and the 10th Bank, let us talk about your father, Daryl Gibbons, also known as Cube. He was wanted for the murder of a transwoman named Silk. A former radio personality, who became homeless after being terminated from her job. She was also known to be a sex worker in this community before being murdered and was found in an abandoned car in the alley behind this restaurant. The FBI was also looking for Daryl Gibbons due to allegations that he was kidnapping teenagers and young girls for Alpha's sex trafficking ring. He was found shot in your basement two years ago. Are you ok with talking about that?" Anna asks.

"Why did she bring that up?" I hear the voice of Bell speak in my ear. Again, he's not real. It's a hallucination. It's not real. I keep reminding myself as I feel anger rising in me because Anna brought up the murder of my father. Something I felt that I had grown from.

"You kind of put me on the spot," I answer with a fake laugh. "My father was not a father to me growing up. He molested me several times, along with my cousin Tina. Tina's father, my uncle Larry Simms, was more of a father to me than my father. A few days after the events of my kidnapping by Bell, I was spending time with my children at the house. I went into the basement to put clothes from the washing machine into the dryer and noticed that my home had been broken into. My father was on the run from the police around this time. I found him hiding in the laundry area. He charged at me with a gun, I snatched it and shot him. The bullet killed him instantly. I'm told that I blacked out for some time after shooting him. I only remember my daughter Desha calling the police and she later told me she stayed with me there on the floor until the police came." I pause and stop myself from smiling.

It is a lie. The truth is Hakeem's brother Jamar gave me that gun for protection due to all the crime in the area. I didn't expect my father to break into my home, but I did feel free from the cloud that had followed me for years. Between his constant molestations, and raping my cousin Tina, which I believe led to her death, I hated him. Nothing brings me greater joy than knowing I ended the nightmare. The night I took Cube's life, I slept like a baby. The State's

Attorney cleared me of all wrongdoing and my life has never been better. If I could have killed my father sooner, I would have. I only wish I had shot him more than once.

"What were you thinking when you pulled the trigger?" Anna asks me as I continue ruminating about the events of that night. I try to remember the stories I told the police officers and Jada Austin. I see Bell evaporate into thin air as I attempt to gather words. My heart begins to pound and my breath feels heavy. I glance at Anna Cartwright, but before I look down I feel a warm hand on my shoulder.

It's another hallucination. I know this because I can clearly hear my grandmother's voice, "It's ok. It's your truth to tell. Not theirs to know." The feeling of her hand quickly dissipates. The warmth from her voice in my ear is nonexistent. I sense Anna Cartwright's impatience.

"I was scared," I answer. "I'd heard rumors about my father working with the Alphas. I know what he did not tell me, I know what he did to my cousin Tina. I also know the effects of what he did to her. My cousin, Tina Simms took her life following the rape. I had no idea what my father was going to do to me or my children. He broke into my home with a gun pointed at me. I did what any other mother would do. I protected my nest. My grandmother's home was a safe place for me growing up. That's part of the legacy of the home. It will always continue because I made sure that day that it was a safe place for my children."

"Is there anything you would like to leave with the viewers of this program?" Anna asks as one of the members of the camera crew points to his watch.

"Protect your children at all costs. This world has monsters that hide behind the faces of rapists, molesters and people who protect them. The last thing you want to live with is regret. I regret that I wasn't able to protect my cousin Tina from my father. I regret that my youngest daughter Kenya was killed in a hit-and-run car accident. I regret that my oldest two children's father was murdered in prison and is not present in their lives. I regret that my son, RJ's, father has life in prison. I regret that I can't tell anyone who Trinity's father is. Most of all, I regret that my children had to watch me struggle. But every bit of my struggling was to make the best life for them. The place we call home, I protect it. This restaurant, I use the income to provide for them. I thank God for the sacrifices my grandmother made. Leaving me a home and money from her insurance policy so that I could open this restaurant. To my single mothers out there, don't stop grinding. Get work done. Provide for these kids. Don't leave anything up to no man, no woman, no judge, no politician. Leave it up to yourself. And before you die, make sure you have something to leave your children. And I'm not talking about bills, bad credit and trauma like my mother Linda Gibbons did."

"Cut!" a producer yells.

Chapter 2

Later that evening, my 13-year-old twins Desha and Darrin are sitting on one of the couches in the living room as Hakeem and I sit on the love seat watching the news. Two African American anchors, Ebony and Horace, are seated with the letters A, F, and K to their left.

"Tonight we have more news coming from out of the Ridgely Square Community," Ebony states as Darrin, who was playing on his phone places it between him and Desha, before scooting closer to the end of his seat to look at the TV screen. "Police Commissioner Junior Dawson has confirmed another homicide victim. This is now the 12th victim in 3 days. Commissioner Junior Dawson was able to confirm that all 12 victims were related to the Action Figure Killer, also known as AFK. If you all remember, AFK sent a letter to this station a few weeks ago, calling himself by that name, and stating that he is going after members of the gang called the Alphas. No other details were provided by Baltimore City Police."

"It's interesting that the police department hasn't called him a serial killer," Horace chimed in.

"What do you mean?" Ebony asks as she turns slightly towards Horace but still faces the camera.

"The police have identified 12 murders from AFK in the last 3 days in this community. The victims are said to be members of the Alpha gang, but they are not considering this AFK person a serial killer? Why?" Horace asks as Ebony slowly shakes her head in agreement.

"Some of the victims of AFK were identified as sex workers associated with the Alpha gang. As many of you may remember, the possibility of the Alphas running a sex trafficking ring was called into question. There is still an ongoing investigation in relation to the Alphas being involved in a sex trafficking ring," Ebony states as Horace glances directly into the camera.

"Yes, and let us not forget, this all came out after the investigation of the Narcotics and Firearms Task Force was called into question two years ago. NAFA was a task force created by the former Baltimore City Police Commissioner, Alex Tillman, who was relieved of his duties three years ago following an angry outburst at reporters and residents of Baltimore City concerning the deaths of two African American teenagers, Kennard Lyles-Bey and Tyrone Clinton."

"Which is understandable," Horace continues. "Kennard Lyles-Bey was shot and killed by a Baltimore City Police Officer after spray painting on a building. Tyrone Clinton was shot and killed following a failed attempt at an armed robbery. Many citizens became upset following Tyrone Clinton's murder because video footage showed the young man surrendering to police before he was shot. Officer Edward Carter, who happened to be Tyrone Clinton's football coach, went to visit Kennard Lyles-Bey at the hospital and was attacked by two Alpha gang members and was murdered. Commissioner Alex Tillman was on the scene during this event and returned fire, killing the two gang members."

Ebony held her hand up towards Horace in a motion for him to continue his elaborating as Horace turned towards the camera. "We don't need to stay on this subject for too long, but during the court case of Marshawn Bell, who was a detective and leader of NAFA, stated that he hired the two Alpha members to kill Officer Edward Carter. Alex Tillman learned of this, and followed Bell after his deal made in court to provide information related to the sex trafficking ring. Marshawn Bell kidnapped a resident to accompany him and his mother to go to Virginia where Alex Tillman rescued the woman and killed Marshawn Bell…"

"…In other news," Ebony says, adjusting her chair and moving papers around on her desk, "Baltimore City Councilman Dawson, stated that he is stepping down from office effective immediately. He made a brief statement on social media today that he wanted to support his son, the current Baltimore City Police Commissioner, Junior Dawson."

Hakeem turns towards me and lowers the volume on the television as the twins leave out of the living room. Sounds from RJ playing his keyboard upstairs enter into the living room. "I should run for his seat!" Hakeem says with excitement as I watched Darrin walk out of the house with a zip down hoodie on.

"Why?" I ask. Maybe not the best choice of words, but this totally came from out of nowhere.

"Hear me out, Tiff. We have the 10th Bank fighting for this community. We have my brother Jamar fighting to make this community sovereign. We are trying to win this war against Titan Industries. What better way to end this fight than to get elected to the office that gave them an initial green light to take over this district. Councilman Dawson has done more to hurt this district than anyone I can name."

"So you think he did more damage than Marshawn Bell?" I ask as I notice a figment-like image of Bell appear behind Hakeem, shaking his head in an up-and-down motion with a giant smirk on his face.

"I don't know how to answer that one. I mean, Bell did shoot me, and he kidnapped you. But getting this position would be a step in the right direction to solidify Pastor Avery's and your grandmother's life's work. It could save this district," Hakeem states as I shake my head no.

"We have the 10th Bank. We have the church. We have my restaurant. We have your brother's mosque and the community center. We have more and more community agencies joining us. We don't need the city council to do anything," I rebut as there's a knock on the door.

I open the door to find Jamar standing there with a smile on his face. "I don't know if you all heard but Councilman Dawson is stepping down," he says, walking into the house and hugging his brother, Hakeem.

"This is a huge step in the right direction, right?" Hakeem asks as Jamar nods in agreement.

"Your brother wants to run for his seat," I interject as Jamar's facial expression turns to a serious one.

"Why?" Jamar asks as Hakeem sits back on the love seat. He gently grabs my hand and slightly tugs it for me to sit next to him. I do. I can now smell the scent of his cologne. It is a very light, pleasant scent.

"We can win the fight against Titan Industries. We can save the schools that Councilman Dawson and Titan Industries have tried to cut out the budget and destroy. We can make Ridgely Square great again!" Hakeem exclaims.

"Dude, why are you yelling? Are the kids still up?" Jamar asks.

"Desha is in the other room. RJ and Trinity are upstairs playing with the keyboard and drums you bought them," I answer.

"Where's Darrin?" Jamar asks.

"He just went outside with some of his friends, I guess. I'm surprised you didn't pass him on the way here," I answer.

"Not trying to tell you and Hakeem what to do, but be careful with having him going out after dark and hanging out like that. The Alphas are going crazy, the Cabal are becoming more present in Ridgely Square since NAFA has been wiped off the board and we have a serial killer on the loose," Jamar states.

"The serial killer, AFK?" I ask.

"Yes," Jamar answers, rolling his eyes in a playful manner. "He's killing people associated with the gang now, but it's just a matter of time before he gets bored with that and starts aiming at other people." Jamar pauses for a second before stating, "…or she. AFK could be a woman."

"That is true," I answer, leaning into Hakeem's shoulder.

"Aside from that, Hakeem, we have a lot going on. You have a lot going on. Are you sure that you want that added responsibility. The term will be up next year anyway. We need to focus on getting away from anything related to how things have been, and make our own government and structure. The 10th Bank is a major step in that direction, and it's working," Jamar states. "Why not have Sasha do it? People love her. Think about it. Her son was murdered by police, she's intelligent, she was displaced by Titan Industries, she–"

"She's inpatient at a substance abuse clinic," I interject. "Sorry to cut in. Sasha has been inpatient for a while. Between the murder of her son, Tyrone, having someone killed in front of her by Marshawn Bell and all the other stress she has endured, her alcohol usage got out of hand."

"I saw the lights on at Gina's house, is Gina out of witness protection?" Jamar asks.

"No, the FBI still has Gina in witness protection for the sex trafficking investigation. Mya started renting the unit from Gina, and basically has the whole house to herself now that Sasha is in rehab," I answer.

"Mya who?" Jamar asks, sitting down on Darrin's gaming chair that has recently become more of a waste of space than an item that is of use in the house.

"Mya Rodriguez," Hakeem answers. "The community activist that lived in the Arts District. She did a lot of work getting anti-discrimination laws passed for the LGBTQ population in the Maryland General Assembly. She also got the funding to reopen the Jasper Theater in the Arts District, not sure if you remember but that cost about $180 million."

"How did she do that?" Jamar asks, turning on Darrin's PlayStation and changing the TV to the gaming channel.

"She networked with this group of investors called the Flamingo Club. A bunch of old money philanthropists in Baltimore that invest in projects to bring life back into the historic Baltimore areas," Hakeem answers, grabbing the controller. The two brothers pick a football game to play.

It's funny how they are both in their 30s, but turn into children when the PlayStation is turned on.

"Do you think we can get the Flamingo Club to invest in the 10th Bank, or partner to salvage the rest of the Old Market Place?" I ask as they both say no simultaneously.

"We're not their cup of tea, Tiff," Hakeem responds. "The Flamingo Club is interested in something way different than we and Titan Industries are. The only reason they haven't partnered with Titan is because Titan wants to destroy Ridgely Square and completely rebuild a whole different community. The Flamingo Club just wants to fix up old Baltimore buildings and monuments and throw masquerades and other types of parties."

"Why not partner with them?" I ask. "The Arts District is doing good. They have all kinds of great stuff going there. Maybe we can set up a meeting with Mya to see what we can work out."

"That's not our mission," Jamar says, pausing the game and turning towards me. "We want to be sovereign. We want to stand on our own. We want to build up this community, and for this community to be for us. They are not us. The same people that can afford to live in The Arts District are some of the same people that Titan wants to live in the rest of Ridgely Square after they finish gentrifying the community. We need this community to be run completely by our people without outsiders investing, and having a stake or say in our community. We follow the plan, we run our schools, our businesses and we dictate our terms. Stay away from the Flamingo Club."

"We should at least try to see if they can help," Hakeem states, kicking the back of Jamar's chair in a playful manner.

"No," Jamar says sternly. "Every major black movement was derailed by outside influences. If you don't learn from the past, you're doomed to repeat it. Trust me. Let them do them. We do us."

"He's right," I hear the disembodied voice of my grandmother speak in my ear.

Chapter 3

Inside of the packed-to-capacity New Hope Greater Love Church, Hakeem gathers several residents of Ridgely Square to talk about the recently opened city council seat. Over the last two years, Hakeem has invested money into renovating the church, including painting the walls, putting down new carpet, fixing the windows, updating the pews and installing central air conditioning.

"Ladies and gentlemen, we need to move forward to the Promised Land," Hakeem states walking in front of the pulpit area, standing by a wooden table that is used to serve communion. "Titan Industries plans to move forward with taking your home, your schools, your identity. And why? To build a private college, an outdoor shopping mall, and high end luxury condominiums and homes. They even threatened to knock down this church to turn it into a parking garage. This church, that is the oldest theater for African Americans in the United States. This church was the only place where African Americans could watch motion pictures during the Jim Crow Era. They want to take it away. My brother, an Islamic minister, runs a community resource center and has had his building threatened by Titan. They want to purchase your property, offering lowball prices. Why?"

"The gangs, the drugs, NAFA, the serial killer AFK. Have you seen the news?" an elderly woman screams out from the second row.

"We're fighting against that. The 10th Bank has created a collection of community leaders, stakeholders, and religious leaders to fight back, but we need to go further," Hakeem answers. "My advocacy group, Justice 4 All, is now a joint partnership effort with the Baltimore City Police Department and the 10th Bank. We can go further than that. There's a special election coming up for Councilman Dawson's seat. If I am elected to that position, we can fix this community. We can continue to take it back."

"Why can't you do it from where you are now?" a short Latin American woman says, standing up in the rear of the church. She appears to be in her early 40s, with long brunette hair, and a slim build. She is wearing ripped jeans and a blue Adidas T-shirt.

"You don't know how, that's why," she says, walking closer to Hakeem. I begin to feel uncomfortable with the exchange between the two. "Hi. My name is Mya Rodriguez. I'm a community activist that has gotten things done. In the Arts District, I worked to get bills passed, and fixed a theater many thought was gonna be demolished, or would continue being abandoned. I looked around all of Ridgely Square, and what did I see? Vacant houses, drug addicts, drug dealers, sex workers, murder victims, people living in trauma, people living in fear, poverty. I saw the property values going down. What should be a family's legacy, your home, is now a family's burden. Why is that? Because of people like Dr. Andrews. They mean well, but they want another title instead of wanting to do the work. Dr. Hakeem Andrews runs the 10th Bank, they're doing great work, I know. Dr. Hakeem Andrews runs Justice 4 All, and has improved the relationship between the community and the police department. Here's my problem. What community? I work with young people that are Gay, Lesbian and Transgender. I don't see you fighting for them. Several sex workers have been killed, maybe by this Action Figure Killer, maybe by the Alphas, I don't know. But I don't see you fighting for them. I don't see you talking to Junior Dawson demanding answers, making sure we are all safe. I don't see you talking to your new cop buddies and asking them to get the FBI in here to explore if AFK is a serial killer. I'm here to publicly announce my candidacy for the city council position. I vow, if elected, to make Ridgely Square safer for all. I vow to lower the crime rate in Ridgely Square, I vow to make Ridgely Square a place where Latinx, African American, LGBTQ, and Asian Americans can call home. I vow to continue the dream of Pastor Donald Avery and Mother Florence Simms. I would like to talk to each one of you about my plans going forward with the community.”

Instantly, I grow angry. She used my grandmother's name in her pitch. She didn't know my grandmother. I walk out the worship hall area and into the children's church area where a slim built man wearing a black suit is standing next to another man wearing a black and white Nike jacket and jeans.

“Tiffany Gibbons, correct?” the man in the black suit asks as I nod to confirm. “My name is Paul. I was hoping to speak to you and your fiancé.”

“About what?” I ask in fear. There's something about Paul's and his associate's faces that is unsettling.

“I want to work with you and your fiancé to build up the community. You all do a lot of work in Ridgely Square. The 10th Bank has become a huge success. You're featured in articles, getting interviews, and even run a restaurant. I want to know when would be a good time to meet."

Soon as Paul finished his sentence, Hakeem opened the door to the children's church room. The gentleman standing next to Paul reached to his side and pulled out a gun as Paul motioned with his right hand for the man to lower his gun. The man showed no sign of fear, didn't appear startled by Hakeem entering the room, but was ready to shoot. He had a blank expression.

"Did I ruin something?" Hakeem asks, startled by what he just witnessed. "We normally don't hold up in a children's church with guns. Especially with my fiancée present."

"We don't mean any harm, Dr. Andrews. With everything going on in Ridgely Square, Roland here didn't want to take any chances," Paul answers with a smile on his face. The smile did not seem happy or joyful. It was the least comforting expression I have ever seen. I was once kidnapped at gunpoint by a person that laughed and joked a lot and he appeared more joyful.

"What can we help you guys with?" Hakeem asks as I move closer towards him.

"Again," Paul states, "I want to invest my money into the 10th Bank. Titan Industries wants to destroy everything in Ridgely Square. I'm firmly against that. I also see that you all are building up the community with all the black owned companies. I am very much for that. Where can I fit in?"

"What do you do?" Hakeem asks as Paul chuckles.

"Ask your brother about me, Dr. Andrews. We'll give you some time to talk it over." Paul and Roland walk past Hakeem and I and leave the children's church room. Hakeem lets out a loud exhale as a very light skinned woman, that is about 5 foot 11 inches walks into the room.

Hakeem and I look at each other and then back at the woman, noticing it is Erica Little, one of the executives for Titan Industries. Erica and her husband Sedrick Little are in charge of Titan Industries' Urban Development Program. Since the murder of their child, Silk, Erica and Sedrick have been in the middle of a rocky separation and possible impending divorce. A large portion of their marital problems were based around Silk's identity as a transwoman and how they handled her death.

"I'm so glad I caught you," Erica says, looking at Hakeem and me. "This community has gone way downhill since the last time I was here."

"The last time you were here, as in Ridgely Square, was about three to four years ago at the funeral home. You were getting run out for showing up at Pastor Avery's wake, and being exposed for disowning your child for being a transgender," Hakeem states, stepping towards Erica Little.

"That was my husband's decision," Erica says, rolling her eyes in a dismissive fashion. "Nevertheless, Simon Little, or should I say Silk, is dead. She's still dead. My actual daughter, Sabrina, is still dead as well. I can't change any of that. I wish I could. But that is not why I'm here."

"Why are you here?" I ask as Erica walks closer to me and looks closely at my shirt.

"Making a deal," Erica answers. "Titan Industries would love to work with every citizen of Ridgely Square. We would love to work with the 10th Bank. That restaurant of yours, Legacy of Florence, we would love to work with that too. Here's the deal. The property values here have continued to decrease. NAFA didn't do you all any favors. The riots resulting from those two kids that were murdered, again, didn't do you all any favors. The investigation into the sex ring, and the drug dealing by the Alphas and the Cabal. It continues to make this place less desirable. Here's where we come back in. We're willing to make offers. Y'all can sell properties and move on. Get something better. We'll fix this place up."

"And if we can't, can we come back into one of the newer places?" Hakeem asks.

"Maybe, if you can afford it. We want to do planned communities," Erica answers. "A certain look that meshes with the vision. Pastor Avery was someone that looked into the past for the answers. I'm giving you the future. Trust me on this. One way or another it's going to happen."

"It's not, and we're seeing to it," I answer as Erica places her hand on my shoulder.

"Tiffany. You remember when we first met at the community center? I offered you an option to get a voucher in Baltimore County. You said no, the building you were living in was purchased by Titan and demolished. You and your children moved into your grandmother's house. But that's not the whole story, is it?"

"What are you talking about?" I ask, puzzled as to where she was going. I knew she couldn't possibly know about the money Bell gave me.

"When I gave you a way out this ghetto, you said no. A short time later your daughter and your baby father were killed in a hit and run," Erica says as I ball up my fist in an attempt to hit her. Before I can raise my arm, she gently places her hand over my balled fist in a non-threatening motion.

"I also lost my daughter Sabrina to a hit and run," Erica continues. She looks down and appears to have tears in her eyes. There is legit sadness on her face. Something I never thought I would see from this woman.

"Why? Why are you telling me this?" I ask as Hakeem places his arm around me to comfort me.

"We both lost our children to senseless violence. Decades apart, but the same kind of death. Hit-and-runs. But the deaths in this city aren't just hit-and-runs. Simon, or should I say Silk, was murdered by your father. It was so hard for Silk to find a job that he started prostituting in the Old Market Place area. That wouldn't have happened if Baltimore had a better economy. This city needs to go in Titan's direction."

"Your direction is only beneficial to the upper middle class," Hakeem chimes in. "None of your plans are designed to benefit families that make less than $120K a year. I saw the proposals, remember?"

"The college students will be able to stay in the dorms. That will be affordable, Dr. Andrews," Erica answers. "The money to make a better Baltimore has to come from somewhere. You two own a bank, you know that. But it's time for a major change in this community. Let's play Ridgely Square Bingo. I'm going to name a few problems off. If you can agree Ridgely Square has 5 of these problems, yell out, *Bingo.*"

"Please stop," Hakeem says in a serious tone. He and I are quickly becoming annoyed by Erica.

"Just bear with me," Erica says as we hear people walking through the hallway of the church. "A crooked police task force named NAFA, gangs, vacant houses, murdered sex workers, sex trafficking orchestrated by the gangs, drugs, a rising murder rate, a serial killer that nobody wants to call a serial killer. Did anybody get bingo yet?"

"What do we win if we say Bingo?" the disembodied voice of Bell says in my ear.

"It's time for a change. You guys have been fighting change and it keeps getting worse. You two are about to get married. Is this really what you want for your family? Tiffany, you have your grandmother's home. Awesome. Sell it. You two can find somewhere nice and really live a better life. I'm not your enemy here. Reality is," Erica says, walking out of children's church leaving Hakeem and me to look at each other.

Chapter 4

A few days later, Hakeem and I are sitting at a table in my restaurant, enjoying coffee and watching the breakfast crowd funnel inside the restaurant. Since the buzz about the restaurant has grown, the breakfast and dinner crowds have become a steady stream.

Sadly Councilman Dawson noticed the traffic as well, and theorized that placing parking meters in the Old Market Place area would capitalize on the large number of patrons that park there. I hope that idea went out the door with Councilman Dawson. Yet Baltimore City as a whole has a long history of taxing the African American communities. How? you may ask. Here's a brief history over the last 5 years. Baltimore City invested in placing speed and red light cameras in the predominantly black neighborhoods.

The cameras solved zero murder cases. Baltimore City also placed taxes on liquor, bottle caps, plastic bags, added a gas tax, an energy tax to the light bill, and potato chip taxes, along with higher water bills than every other county in the state. Guess who those taxes affect? You guessed it, Black people. I forgot to mention that the taxes are in addition to the $.06 on every dollar you spend in this city.

"The whole time I stood up there talking, I never saw Erica Little sitting in the crowd. I should have spoken in the pulpit," Hakeem states as I turn my gaze from the customers to him. I have three new people working as waiters today, along with my regular staff. The cooks, the servers, the greeters, and the cleaners are all part of the normal crew. This is a busy time of day for the restaurant, so it's easy to get distracted by what's going on. I haven't even been in the market this morning.

"No, you were right, Hakeem. This wasn't a Sunday morning service. You were just speaking to the community about some of the issues," I respond as I notice the young man I just promoted to manager, walk through the door. He's two hours late, and we have new staff people. Would I be wrong if I reprimanded him? He's a 22-year-old undergrad student at Morgan State University. He's really smart, but his lateness is almost unbearable.

"The deal that Titan Industries put in motion with Councilman Dawson for the schools, it's still happening. They're trying to close the schools at the end of this school year. The School Board has been very quiet about the whole thing. The only thing that might be able to hold things up would be me winning the election," Hakeem states in a low tone.

"Or, we use the 10th Bank and invest in one of the applicants to open new schools in the district. We create a curriculum and we do better than the schools that are already here. I would put my kids in one of our own funded schools in a heartbeat," I answer as Hakeem pulls out his smart phone.

"Your tax dollars already fund the schools here. Plus, it would take time to get the schools up and running. You factor in the permits, building, hiring and any other accommodations and we might be two to five years out before an elementary, middle and high school would be fully functional. We have a right now problem. It's April. The special election is being rumored to be in late June. I can push for an extension for the schools to remain open and add them to the budget for the 2019-2020 school year. The Baltimore City-wide election is in early 2020. I can make plans to ensure that the schools stay funded without challenges after I win re-election. It's a realistic plan."

"Hakeem. I love you, and I support you. But why does this have to be you? Why now? Why can't someone like Mya or Jamar do this?" I ask. "Why can't you focus on the 10th Bank, Justice 4 All, and the church? Not to mention we have a wedding we're trying to plan for in 2020."

"I don't buy into Mya's agenda. I don't think it's in the best interest of everybody here. My brother, Jamar, can't run. His criminal record alone would disqualify him. Can you imagine him in a debate talking about isolating Ridgely Square and succession from European Imperial Oppression? He would get slaughtered. The media would have a field day with him," Hakeem states as I try to think of words to say. I feel bad because I actually agree with him about Jamar. I do not know much about Mya. I did not like that she referenced my grandmother like she knew her.

"What did you find out about Paul?" I ask as Hakeem looks down. His face appears glum.

"It's not good, Tiff. Paul Douglass is the highest-ranking Alpha member in Maryland. He has been trying to funnel his money through black-owned companies, the methadone center by your house, and a couple of the churches for years. He was a person of interest for several drug trafficking and distribution charges, but nothing ever stuck. Jamar said that Paul was the one who started the Alphas with sex trafficking. He has been watched like a hawk because of this whole investigation," Hakeem says slowly, looking up at me before placing his hands over mine as they rest on the black table.

"This is bad," I state, and look around the room.

"I know. He has funneled a large portion of his money through his clothing line, Alpha Males," Hakeem continues as a beautiful, light brown skinned, muscular framed woman in a blue pantsuit, who has her hair in a ponytail, sits down at our table. A very recognizable face, the Baltimore City State's Attorney, Jada Austin.

"To what do we owe this pleasure?" Hakeem asks, with a shocked look on his face. Stunned that she sat at our table unannounced and without permission.

"I just wanted to have coffee with a friend," Jada Austin says with a smile. "These coffee beans, where are they from?"

"The Gullah Gullah Island," I answer, feeling nervous. I feel my stomach turning in knots as Jada Austin looks at me. I'm not sure if she is going to ask me about the money I took from Marshawn Bell two years ago or tell me that my aunt Gina was murdered. It's amazing how many people related to the sex trafficking case were murdered over the last few years. The media didn't connect all the murders to AFK, but I had my theories.

"I order it every time I come here. It's delicious," Jada adds, as one of the waiters comes to the table to take her order for coffee. The waiter shortly returns to the table with a coffee cup and pours a fresh cup of coffee for her.

When the waiter walks away, Jada glances at Hakeem briefly before looking back in my direction.

"You're so tense. I'm not here to bring charges," Jada jokes. "I do have some questions, though. It's about your father, Daryl Gibbons. Did you know that he was working for the Alphas?"

"I heard rumors, but nothing for sure. We didn't have a good relationship," I answer as Jada nods in agreement.

"Again, you're not in trouble for anything. Take a deep breath. The Alphas aren't a local gang like the Ridgely Homes Boys or the Cabal. The Alphas have moved into almost every metropolitan region. Your father was said to be one of the people to grab many young girls then ship them off to a different state. Around the time that Marshawn Bell took the plea deal for his freedom, a burn list was made for several Alpha members, sex workers, informants and customers. Did you know any of that?"

"No. I have nothing to do with that case. That was my aunt Gina's wheelhouse. I couldn't care less," I answer as Jada peers into my eyes.

"Did you ever look at the information on the USB drive your aunt Gina gave to you to give to the FBI?" Jada asks. I shake my head no. "A lot of the names on one or both of the USB drives were involved in sex trafficking and drug distribution. I'm talking heroin, Fentanyl and powdered cocaine. The Alpha's burn list appears to include anyone that would or did talk to the FBI during the current investigation."

"Why not offer witness protection to the people on the list like you did for Aunt Gina," I ask as Jada chuckles.

"It don't work like that, hun. A lot of the people on that list are bad people. Many of whom have warrants and are involved in other investigations. Your aunt Gina Simms was cleared of any wrongdoing. She provided a lot of great information for the NAFA case and this sex trafficking case. So I want to ask you again, did you know that your father was working with the Alphas?"

"No," I answer emphatically.

"Did you, or have you ever worked with the Alphas?" Jada asks. I shake my head no. She turns to Hakeem as he shakes his head no as well. "I figured you two didn't. My only problem is I heard about your community meeting a couple days ago. I also heard that Paul Douglass was there. The same Paul Douglass who is the head of the Alphas. The same Paul Douglass under investigation for embezzlement, sex trafficking, extortion, bribery, murder, and countless other cases. Why was he at your church, Dr. Andrews?"

"He wanted to discuss getting more involved in the 10th Bank," Hakeem answers as Jada glances at the two of us.

"I know you're telling the truth. There's nothing about this whole situation that makes me concerned. What you should be concerned about is Paul having interest in you. I know you're running for office and have the bank. You're trying to help the community. Paul is a cancer to these people. He will be brought to justice. The former commissioner, Alex Tillman tried his damnedest and failed numerous times. I think this investigation is going to stick. But Paul is using this burn list to ensure his freedom. If you cross him, I wouldn't be shocked if he tried to kill you too."

"Do you think Paul hired the Action Figure Killer to kill off anyone that could testify against him?" Hakeem asks as Jada throws her hands in the air signaling that she doesn't know.

Jada finishes drinking her cup of coffee, then looks at Hakeem and me and says, "Stay far away from Paul and even farther away from this whole investigation. Don't contact your aunt Gina, don't do anything related to the Alphas. Dr. Andrews, I would encourage you to distance Paul Douglass from your campaign. Last thing we need is another crooked politician."

Jada places $10 on the table next to her receipt and walks out of the restaurant. Moments later I hear Bell's voice in my ear laughing.

"You know what's funny about Jada Austin?" Bell's voice asks. "She's actually a crooked politician. She withheld evidence related to sex trafficking to further her career. She let me work with the Alphas and turned a blind eye as long as I made her conviction numbers look good on paper. Now she wants to dictate what you can and can't do. She's free to practice law, I'm dead and you got out of a murder charge, thanks to her. So you benefited as well. I wonder what's her angle?"

"I have to get over to the office, my brother is waiting on me," Hakeem says before kissing me and walking out of the restaurant.

Chapter 5

Later that evening, I am sitting at one of the booths inside of the restaurant with my 11-year-old daughter Trinity and my 10-year-old son RJ. The place is packed for dinner as usual. Several of my staff members appear tired, annoyed, and two of them appear to be under the influence of marijuana. The two kids from the high school always sneak off towards the close of business to smoke weed behind the dumpsters, then sneak back in and actually believe nobody notices. Those are the two people I chose to wash the dishes. What was I thinking?

To my surprise, Mya walks into the restaurant and sits by the bar area. She glances towards me several times, attempting to get my attention and eventually I oblige. I sit next to her as the television behind the bar plays reruns of Good Times.

"I really like what you did to this building," Mya states as one of the bartenders walks towards her. The young lady notices me sitting next to Mya and makes her way a little quicker than normal. Mya orders two shots of tequila before turning her attention back towards me. "I hope you're able to get the rest of this outdoor mall back open."

"That's the goal," I say as the bartender returns with her two shot glasses filled with alcohol. "It's one day at a time."

"Your fiancé, does he like to be called Dr. Andrews, Reverend Andrews, Reverend Hakeem, or Pastor Andrews? I really don't want to be disrespectful," Mya asks before downing the first shot of tequila.

"He doesn't get caught up with all the titles. You can just call him Hakeem, and he'd be happy. What would you like to be called," I ask. A smirk immediately shoots across her face.

"Mya is fine. Hakeem is very well connected to this community. To Baltimore as a whole, to be honest. I know going against him is going to be a tough task, and I want him to know this is nothing personal."

"I don't think he or anyone else thinks that you running in this election is anything personal," I interject.

"Like you and Hakeem, I'm also a minority. A triple minority. I'm Latinx, I'm openly gay and I'm a woman. I represent the population that is often overlooked in these elections. Hakeem represents, again no disrespect, the population that gets the wrong kind of attention or is often ignored. I don't want to be the politician that is just for a specific group. I want to be the person that is for all the groups."

I gestured towards the bartender to bring Mya another shot as she drank the second glass of tequila. "Mya, what you have done in the Arts District is incredible. There is no debate in that. Hakeem is just doing what he feels is right for the whole district. Look behind me. My two youngest children are doing homework for a school that might be shut down at the end of this school year. Then they will have to go to new schools, deal with new teachers and possibly new problems. Baltimore is in the middle of a gang war, thanks to what Marshawn Bell and NAFA did two years ago. I don't know what those gangs are doing in the community where my kids may go to school next. I know what's going on in this one."

"What's your point?" Mya asks as the bartender brings her another shot glass and Mya asks for a glass of rum and coke.

"My point is, this part of Ridgely Square is facing problems that your side isn't," I answer.

"I live on the Ridgely Homes side too, now. You do know I'm renting your aunt's house," Mya states as I shake my head.

"I may have said that wrong. You did a lot of advocacy work in the Arts District. The Ridgley Homes, Ridgley Market Place and School Side all have other challenges. That's what Hakeem is trying his best to represent and fight for."

"How would you feel about hosting a debate here at the restaurant between Hakeem and me? I think it would be good for the residents," Mya says. I glance back at the children to make sure they are doing their homework and not playing on their electronics.

"I wouldn't mind. Either there or the church. There's a community center not too far from here that would be a good place to host it as well," I add.

"What's your stance on sex workers? Do you think that profession should be legalized? Do you think they should be protected?" Mya asks.

"My aunt, your landlord Gina Simms, did sex work for years. Had several run ins with law enforcement. She also had a chemical addiction to opioids. During her time as a sex worker, my aunt became friends with a transwoman known as Silk that was murdered. You may know Silk as being the child of Erica Little from Titan Industries. If sex workers like Gina and Silk were protected, Silk might still be alive today. I do believe they should be protected, just like my staff here, just like the residents of the Arts District," I answer as Mya glances at her phone.

"You do know that I was the reason that police presence was increased in the Arts District," Mya states as she takes a sip of her rum and coke. "Residents that travel to the bars and the lounges in that area feel safe, with a reduced chance of being robbed, shot or murdered. Where we have women that participate in sex work in that area, they feel a lot safer than the rest of Ridgely Square. Imagine what we can do for everyone under my leadership."

"I'm sure Hakeem would like to do the same. His major thing now is trying to reduce the gang activity in the community, and increase home ownership," I respond as Mya hands me the phone.

On the phone is a report that the Baltimore State's Attorney, Jada Austin, was murdered by AFK. It states that he left a note at the scene of the crime, calling himself 'Justice' and stating that Jada Austin worked with Marshawn Bell to cover up crimes by NAFA. The note also says that Jada Austin called herself the 'Silent Partner' of Marshawn Bell during his time working with the Alpha gang and extorting many residents.

The article continues, "The Baltimore City Police Commissioner Junior Dawson has requested that AFK turn himself in. If anyone has any information on the Action Figure Killer, please come forward."

"She was just here," I state to Mya, in shock as I glance back at RJ and Trinity playing on their electronic devices at the booth. I know it will be just a matter of time before they get bored with their school work and start playing.

"I really liked Jada. This is bad," Mya says in a solemn tone.

"Why do they call him the Action Figure Killer?" I ask as I see her face succumb to sadness.

"He leaves a child's toy, some kind of action figure, at the scene of the crime. They didn't call him that. He wrote Nubian Media and the police for them to call him that. I'm sorry, I shouldn't be here," Mya states as she attempts to stand up. I grab her hand requesting that she stay.

"I can see that you're hurt. You must have been really close to Jada," I state as she nods in agreement. The tears begin to flow from her eyes, and the wrinkles in her flawless face become more pronounced.

"We dated for a brief period of time a few years back. I broke it off when she wouldn't come out to her family. I didn't like the fact that I was a secret. What is love if love cannot be shown? How can you say you love me, if you can't be proud that you're with me? What was I thinking? She was a good person. She did everything she could to help the people of the Arts District, even after I treated her like trash. Now. Well I never got to say I'm sorry, or work anything out."

I tell the bartender not to charge Mya for the drinks and to bring me a glass of water. My oldest daughter Desha walks into the restaurant and towards the back booth where RJ and Trinity are still playing. I glance back at Mya who is looking at pictures of Jada Austin on her phone.

"I'm sorry about this, Mya, I truly am. The father of my youngest daughter Kenya and I had a stupid breakup. He tried to find a job for the longest time, but couldn't because of his record. I broke up with him because I found marijuana in the house. He was hiding it from me. I felt that he wasn't taking things as seriously as I wanted him to. I would ask him to purchase milk, or eggs, or cheese. He wouldn't have money. Yet, he had this giant bag of weed hidden in the apartment. So I snapped. Every time I had the chance to fix it, and work on our relationship, I let my pride get in the way. Then one day, boom, he and my daughter were killed in a hit and run. They never caught the guy that hit the car."

"Are you saying, they're never going to catch AFK?" Mya asks, barely looking at me.

"No, that's not what I'm saying. I'm sorry, I'm not the speech person, that's Hakeem. What I'm saying is, this sucks. But I'm here if you need a friend," I respond. Wait, are we friends? I don't know this person. Sasha and I have been friends since middle school. I don't know this lady at all, aside from her trying to run against my fiancé in an election. What am I doing? While I sit in silence with Mya, the TVs in the bar area quickly change to the news reports of Jada Austin's murder. It seems like the letters A, F and K keep repeating every few seconds and becoming an unbearable sound to Mya who has her face down on the bar and her hands folded around her forehead, displaying the tattoos on her arms. Something that she's always covered ever since I've known her.

"Things are about to get real," Bell's voice says in my ear, as I look back towards my children once again that are playing on their electronics.

Chapter 6

A few days later, Desha, RJ, Trinity and I were at the basketball court around the corner from the house. It's a full-size gravel court, with glass and cigarette butts littered throughout. Attached to the court is a small playground. The basketball court has bent rims, graffiti on the backboard and missing nets that most hoops have. Every time the community replaces them, they wind up missing in a few days. Also, the color to the 3 point line is long gone. You can barely make out the free-throw line.

"Some things never change," Erica Little says walking onto the basketball court where Desha is taking a shot, while being guarded by RJ.

"What do you mean?" I ask, shocked that Erica Little would come to the basketball court. I am also confused as to why she is here.

"This court, it has been and will always be a dump. Someone should do something about it. Oh, that's right, that's what I've been trying to do," Erica says as a group of teenage boys walk to the other side of the basketball court, laughing and pointing at me.

"Hold on, Ms. Little. Hey guys, is something going on?" I ask the group of boys as one walks towards my children and me. The kid is very dismissive of Erica Little.

"We know who you are, Ms. Tiffany," the tallest boy says. He is dressed in a red Adidas sweatsuit, dribbling a basketball while the others in his entourage are passing a blunt back and forth. "We respect you. You went up against the Alphas and NAFA and won. We got your back if you ever need us."

"And who are you?" Erica asks as the young man rolls his eyes and looks back to me.

"I'm Moose. But we're the Cabal. You're safe with us," Moose says walking away.

"I don't need your safety," I respond.

"That's not what we heard. Trust me, we don't want anything in return. We just want to make sure that y'all are safe. That's what family do," Moose says, walking with his crew to the playground area where they continue to smoke and talk.

"Sorry about that, Mrs. Erica, or is it Mrs. Little?" I ask as Erica shrugs off my comments.

"You can just call me Erica. I had a speech all planned out. I think I'm going to skip that. I didn't expect to run into a rival gang of the Alphas today. Yet, here you are, in the middle of a drug and turf war," Erica says in a condescending tone. I feel rage and anger as she makes those statements. Her voice still irritates me to this day. My grandmother used to say never wish death on anybody, but I wish AFK could add this one to the list, just saying.

"Your community is changing, Tiffany. It's not the same place that Pastor Avery and Mother Florence Simms grew up in. It's not the same place I lived in for a period of time. It's not the same place you grew up in. On the bright side of things, Baltimore is trying to correct its course. There's going to be bike lanes throughout the city within the next three years. Zoning laws are being passed now to make this city more inhabitable. Property values will be going through the roof. But this has to change to insure progress," Erica says pointing at the playground, the basketball court, and the houses that surround us.

"Your grandmother left you something to live in. She left you with a testament of African American history. A cornerstone to the community. Yet the community she left you in doesn't have those same African American people.

Now it has low income, welfare recipients, gang members, renters and addicts. This is what you want to raise your children in?"

"Keep my kids out your mouth," I chime back as Erica smirks.

"You have your restaurant and the 10th Bank. In theory, you're doing great. You made it. While I'm happy for you, your own family is not," Erica says, pointing at a black Audi with black tinted windows parked by the basketball court.

The passenger's door opens and out steps a medium brown skinned woman with a curly wig, jeans and a sweater. Of course it is my mother of all people. As she walks towards me I notice she is sweating profusely. Linda has a history of high blood pressure and never did herself any favors with her bad habit of eating unhealthy food. With a haughty attitude she continues walking till she's standing next to Erica. I watch Desha, RJ, and Trinity hug her as I start to notice changes in her physical appearance. I haven't seen Linda Gibbons since my grandmother's funeral three years ago.

"What are you doing here? The last I heard, you were doing taxes in Arizona," I state as Linda—I refuse to call her *mom*—plays with Trinity's hair.

"That's true. I'm here because Thaddeus Simms left that house for my mother, Florence, along with her siblings. Florence willed you that house without consulting the family. While speaking with her surviving siblings, we agreed it would be in the family's best interest to sell the home to Titan, and collect," Linda says as Erica smiles and walks back to her car.

"Why?" I ask. "They live in Arizona and Texas. What would it benefit them to sell the house?"

"I'm not here to argue with you, Tiffany. I see you're doing well. I will say that this isn't personal. The family thought it would be in their best interest to sell the house and make a profit while we still can. They don't think you will make the right, or rational decisions in the best interest of the family house," Linda says as she watches Desha shoot the basketball.

"What do you mean?" I ask as I get ready to punch Linda. The anger boiling in my blood, along with Bell's voice yelling in my ear telling me to assault her, is more than I can take.

"Where to start? You went to college, earned a degree in social work, then quit the hospital you were working at to open a restaurant with the insurance money left to you by my mother. You shot and killed your father, stating that he broke into our family's home. You constantly accused him of raping you, and mentioned on public television that you didn't feel safe around him. You started hanging out with Gina Little, a person who admitted that she orchestrated a robbery and the murder of your uncle, my brother, Larry. Just so Gina could purchase drugs. Do you see a pattern here? You can't be trusted with decision-making. You're worse than my mom, and at least Florence had Alzheimer's for an excuse."

"Slap this bitch!" Bell screams in my ear.

"You're an embarrassment," I state, overcome with anger and trying to fight back the desire to hurt Linda.

"You are the embarrassment," Linda returns. "You had 5 kids, by 4 different fathers. Desha and Darrin's father, murdered in prison, RJ's father, in prison for murder, Kenya and her father, murdered. Who's Trinity's father by the way?" Linda blurted out as she backed away from my swinging distance.

"He's your dead rapist husband, dumbass. He raped me and got me pregnant. Remember, I told you and you wanted to tell me how much of a sin abortion was. Then you urged me not to tell anybody. Then you denied that he did anything," I say, lowering my voice to insure the kids can't hear me.

"That never happened. You're delusional. Just like you were when you was a teenager. Remember you would say that your grandmother would talk to you, when she wasn't even at the house?" Linda asks as I grab her by her sweater. Erica rushes towards us and separates me from Linda.

"I'm not here for you two to fight. I'm here to make a deal. In the best interest of fair business, I think you two should consult with a legal team over the logistics of the house ownership before we go any further," Erica says as she pushes Linda away from me.

"Why didn't you sell the house you and Daryl lived in? You know, the house where Daryl raped me and Tina. You want to talk about Gina causing Uncle Larry to get killed. Why don't you talk about you inviting Tina into your house for Daryl to rape her and cause a suicide," I scream at her as my oldest son, Darrin, greets Moose and his crew before walking onto the basketball court.

"Your father did nothing of that nature to Tina," Linda responds as she attempts to hug Darrin. My oldest son pushes her away and stands at my side, glancing back towards his siblings.

"I'm free from you and him, may he continue to rot. You can go to hell; I hope you don't take too long to join him," I state as I begin to walk away.

"I want you out of that house in 90 days, Tiffany," Linda yells at me as Erica continues to separate her from me.

"Why didn't you sell that house you and Daryl had?" I ask.

"She did, I gave her a great deal," Erica answers.

"Where did you bury your father? I want to pay my respects," Linda says, walking off the court.

"I didn't," I answer as Darrin continues to watch Linda with a stern look on his face. "The Baltimore City Coroner's Office cremated him after I didn't claim his body for a few months. I went back a few months later to get his ashes and dumped them in that sewage drain by where Erica is parked."

"You're lying," Linda screams back.

"No, she's not." Bell laughs in my ear.

"I'm not," I respond. "If you look in that grass across the street, you can find the box that the ashes were in. If you're really lucky, you can see the ball of mucus I spit on the box too."

"You're a miserable little bitch!" Linda screams at me. Darrin attempts to attack her, but Desha stops him.

"No, actually I'm a free, grown, and happy goddess. Raising four great children. With no credit to your input," I rebut as Linda walks back to Erica's car.

"We'll be in touch," Erica says as she walks away.

Chapter 7

A few hours later Jamar, Hakeem, and I are sitting in my living room. Desha sits next to Jamar and hands him a comic book she recently started to draw. Jamar has quickly become the biggest fan of Desha's artwork.

"I spoke with my grandmother's lawyer a few minutes ago. He told me that neither Erica nor Linda can get the house from me. The final will and testament are air-tight. He wants me to stay away from Linda in the event this turns into a court case," I state as Darrin walks by us in a grey designer hoodie headed toward the door.

"Where are you going?" I ask as he rushes away from the doorway.

"Going to play basketball," he says so fast I have to slowly process the words he stated. Hakeem and Jamar smirk at each other before turning back towards me.

"Here's the good news: Erica can't take the house. The bad news is you can't trust your mother," Jamar states while turning his attention back to Desha's comic book.

"I never could," I respond with a low tone. I feel embarrassed to talk about this situation around any of my children. RJ and Trinity are upstairs playing with the keyboard and the drum set, but the incident at the basketball court was too much for them to witness. They should still be allowed to still be children. They shouldn't have to be exposed to the things that Linda exposed me to.

"Does this mean we don't need another place to live?" Desha asks. Everyone in the house says no.

"Your grandmother is just a bad person. She can't help it," I answer. Desha glances back at Jamar, who is making a goofy face to try to break the mood.

"You mean like covering up what your father did to you?" Desha asks. Hakeem and Jamar look on with blank faces. I too am shocked by Desha's statement.

"Yes," I answer. I mean, you can't lie.

The front door opens after a moment of awkward silence and in comes my eldest son, Darrin and my mother Linda, arguing with each other. I am instantly overcome with anger, and charge towards my mother, but I'm stopped by Jamar and Hakeem.

"What are you doing here?" I scream towards Linda.

"This is the family house, not yours," Linda shouts back as Darrin attempts to push her out the front door. "Get your son before he hurts me."

"Get out the house, dumbass," Darrin says, attempting to push my mother with all his might.

"He's right. Get out the house before we put you out," I yell as Hakeem and Jamar continue to hold me back.

"This is not your house. You take your bastard kids and get out of here! One way or another, y'all are going to have to leave," Linda screams.

I break past Hakeem and manage to punch Linda in her jaw, but Jamar holds my left hand to prevent me from hitting her with a combo of punches.

"You going to shoot me like you did your father?" Linda asks me as Darrin punches my mother and kicks her in the knee.

"I don't see why I wouldn't. You're trespassing and I demand that you leave," I scream back at Linda. I notice movement through the still open front door and turn to see three white men standing there, listening in on our conversation. One of the men notice our attention is now turned on them and speaks.

"Sorry to bother you. My name is Agent Dennis Parker of the Federal Bureau of Investigation; we met a couple of years ago. The gentlemen with me are Detective Murphy of the Baltimore City Police Department, and the former Baltimore City Police Commissioner, Alex Tillman. We're here to ask you a few questions," Agent Parker says as my mother looks at my household and me.

Agent Parker is a young chubby white male with short brown hair, wearing a black suit, and no tie. Detective Murphy is a grizzled-early red-haired Irish American cop with a stubble beard, wearing a button up shirt, slacks and dress shoes. He is broad built and tall. Alex Tillman is also broad built, wearing jeans, a tucked in white shirt and dress style boots.

"I was just leaving," Linda says as Detective Murphy blocks the doorway. "Actually, you're the person we want to talk to."

"Is this a good place to talk?" Agent Parker asks with a warm smile. Linda shakes her head no, as we all shake our heads yes, and invite the gentlemen into the house.

"Please, can we go somewhere else?" Linda pleads as I notice her face is covered in sweat.

"She just was saying how this is the family house. Nobody can support you while you talk to law enforcement better than family, right?" Jamar jokes.

"We're not going to hold you long, Mrs. Gibbons," Alex Tillman says in a firm and authoritative tone. "Did you know anything about your husband, Daryl Gibbons, also known as Cube, working for the Alphas?"

My mother shakes her head in denial. "Cube was a good man. He was not any of the things that he was accused of over the years. He just never had anybody to believe in him," Linda states as Darrin shakes his head no.

"I ain't no snitch, but he dead now, so it don't count. He raped my mother and my cousin Tina. They also said he was snatching little girls off the street. It ain't snitching if you telling on predators," Darrin says sizing up Detective Murphy, who appears to be doing the same thing to my eldest son.

"There was a report and DNA that linked Cube to the rape of Ms. Tina Simms. Your deceased niece, right Mrs. Gibbons?" Detective Murphy asks as my mother stands in silence. "Are you able to hear, Mrs. Linda Gibbons? I'm talking to you. Did you know anything about Cube working for the Alphas?"

"Cube was the victim of being a black man, living in this country. He wasn't a child molester, a rapist or some child abductor!" Linda responds as Detective Murphy rolls his eyes.

"Lady please," Detective Murphy responds. "We have Daryl "Cube" Gibbons dead to rights with his DNA on multiple rape victims, not just your niece. Your own daughter, standing right there, has publicly said that he was a rapist. She killed him out of fear of what he may, or may not have done after breaking into this house. So how can you stand there with a straight face and lie to us?"

"I'm not lying. Wait. Why is the former police commissioner with you all?" my mother asks, confused as Hakeem, Jamar and the twins sit down.

"He's providing us intel related to this child abduction case. That was one of the terms of his deal with the State of Virginia, following the murder of the person that kidnapped your daughter. I'm surprised you didn't know that," Agent Parker answers with a very confused face as he looks at my mother.

"Just to be clear. You know nothing about Daryl Gibbons working with the Alphas?" Detective Murphy asks.

"No, I never knew of anything of that nature," Linda answers in a condescending tone.

"Did you ever hide or cover up anything for Daryl Gibbons?" Alex Tillman asks, giving a strong stern look towards Linda.

"Why would I do something like that? Can you leave, please?" Linda responds in an agitated manner.

"If and when you gentlemen go, can you please take her with you? She's not welcome here. Her name is not on the lease here, and she does not receive any mail here," I suggest as Detective Murphy moves to the side, pointing down the steps in my front yard.

"By letter of the law, you have to leave, Ms. Gibbons," Detective Murphy says as my mother mutters words under her breath at me.

"Don't bring your funky ass back here no more, dumbass. She lied to all y'all niggas," Darrin says, taunting my mother.

"Darrin, we don't talk like that in this house," I say as Jamar laughs.

"Oh, my bad. I guess we don't cuss in front of white folks and preachers," Darrin says as Agent Parker laughs very loudly.

Chapter 8

After a couple of weeks, members of the community are seated inside of the New Hope Greater Love church. Mya and Hakeem are standing in front of the church with microphones. The church may have 40 to 45 people in attendance. Hakeem and I anticipated closer to 250 to 275 people in attendance. Nobody from the media is present, and the majority of the audience are stakeholders; such as, the owner of a methadone clinic, the owners of a couple of community health clinics, the owners of a barbershop and hair salon, a couple of pastors, along with a couple of homeowners.

"Friends and neighbors," Mya says confidently to the audience, "my name is Mya Rodriguez, and I'm running against the gentleman to my right, Dr. Hakeem Andrews, for the vacant City Council position. Dr. Andrews is a man I have a lot of respect for. He has done a lot of great things for the people of this community and for Baltimore City at large. That being said, I believe I am better suited for the job."

The audience is very quiet as members of the community appear to look through Mya. I feel sad for Mya because it appears she does not resonate with the community.

"The reason I feel I am best suited for the job is because of my successful work in the Arts District. The work I was able to do with the art schools, both high school and the college. The work I was able to do with the theaters that were falling apart. The work I was able to do to reduce the crime in the Arts District, and of course the work I was able to do to reduce the violent attacks on sex workers in the Arts District. Ridgely Square has seen a rise in murders, including the murders of sex workers."

The silence in the church is eerie. Mya is actually a good person, and it feels like everyone is being dismissive toward her. I feel really bad for her. Hakeem and I sat next to her at Jada Austin's funeral. We didn't talk about politics during the funeral, we were just there for her.

"The death of the sex workers received very little attention," Mya continues. "AFK received attention for killing the Baltimore City State's Attorney, Jada Austin. AFK also received attention for killing several known drug dealers and people associated with sex trafficking. But what if I told you those young girls, the ones that were murdered, possibly by AFK, were victims of the Alphas, and were not doing it because they thought it was fun. What if I told you those young women were having sex for money to pay bills for basic necessities, like clothes, rent and food?"

"The last high profile murder case for a sex worker was for Silk Diamond, also known as Silk Little, who was Erica Little's daughter. The same Erica Little that has been working with Titan to develop this community to become something more. Erica Little has requested to partner with me to help make Ridgely Square a better place. A place that will reduce the murders, make it safe to run, walk or ride a bike. A place safe for people to raise children. A place free from gangs, drugs and forced sex work.

"Friends and neighbors, I request your support in this special election. Not because I feel I'm owed anything but because I have shown I can do what I am tasked with. Like many of you, I am also a minority. Actually, I'm a double minority: I am a Latinx woman and also an openly gay woman. Those two identities have left me with a bull's eye on my back. That doesn't make me stop fighting for you. That doesn't make me create excuses when things fall apart. No. That makes me fight harder. If you all elect me, I promise to fight harder than anyone has ever fought for you. Thank you for your time."

A handful of people clap their hands, clearly out of politeness, as Hakeem nods respectfully to Mya. Hakeem stands and moves to the front of the pulpit as Mya walks over to sit behind him in a chair facing the audience.

"Good afternoon. As many of you know, my name is Dr. Hakeem Andrews. I'm a community leader, acting pastor, fiancé to my beautiful fiancée, and director of the 10th Bank and the Justice 4 All organization." Hakeem stops for a brief moment as the audience breaks out into applause.

"I'm not going to bore everyone here with my accomplishments. To be fair, I have a lot more work to do before I can be proud of anything. That is why I'm running for office. Not because this is a title. Not that I particularly want to do this. To be fair, my brother and my fiancée really don't want me to run for office. Because of the work I'm trying to complete in this community. But with the direction this city has taken, I have to. We have the gangs, such as the Alphas and the Cabal at war over a flooded drug market. We have a growing murder rate. We also have a serial killer known as the Action Figure Killer.

"Ridgely Square needs to be driven in the right direction. That direction is not Mya Rodriguez's direction. She has done a lot for the Arts District, but she has not done anything for the Ridgely Homes, the Old Market Place or School Side."

The majority of the people in attendance begin to clap and cheer Hakeem's statements as he puts his hand up as a gesture of appreciation but requesting that they hold their applause.

"Almost four years ago, a young man named Tyrone Clinton was shot and killed by two police officers when he gave himself up. That event led to high tension in the community, riots, marches, unrest, and the murder of a police officer that was a friend of mine, who was Tyrone Carter's football coach and a member of this church. His name was Edward Carter. After the murder of Edward Carter, another young man, Kennard Lyles-Bey, lost his life in the same hospital where Edward Carter was gunned down. Kennard Lyles-Bey was a classmate of Tyrone Clinton and was murdered by a police officer while he was attempting to spray paint R.I.P. to his dead friend. A police officer who panicked when Kennard attempted to show him Tyrone's final report card. Tyrone had made honor roll that quarter."

People in the audience continued to cheer for Hakeem as he continued to speak. I felt uncomfortable for Mya, who did not elicit the same level of appreciation or support. If I had not gotten to know Mya over the last few days, I would not have cared.

"Why do I bring this up? some of you may wonder," Hakeem continues. "When Tyrone Clinton was gunned down, I asked Mya and her friends in the Arts District to march with me, come to the candlelight vigil with me, or pray with me. They said no. I petitioned the then police chief, Alex Tillman, the then City Councilman Dawson and the Mayor, Regina Sheppard. Mya and her friends petitioned Councilman Dawson for a bike lane. When I asked for a call for peace between the community and the police department after the murder of Officer Carter and Kennard Lyles-Bey, Mya and her friends continued to ask for a bike lane, paper straws and a ban on plastic bags in the city."

The people in attendance gasp and talk among themselves after Hakeem's statements. Mya continues to look stoically at Hakeem, and never changes her facial expression.

"I respect Mya. I hope she and I can continue to work together, build together and one day really call each other friend. I also believe Mya has great intentions. What I don't believe is that Mya understands our needs. While Mya is a double minority, and I could not completely understand or speak on her struggles as a Latinx woman, an openly gay woman and that community, I can speak on this community that this church is in."

The people in attendance erupt in applause after Hakeem makes that statement. Even with fewer than 50 people in attendance, the cheers are deafening.

"I can speak on the challenges of not knowing where money is coming from, I can speak on the challenges of the taxes, I can speak on the challenges of the mandated bike and bus lanes on our streets that have taken away a lot of parking spots. I can speak on the food deserts, I can speak on the health disparities, I can speak on NAFA, the Alphas and actually advocating for justice to be brought towards the murder of Silk Diamond. Silk's mother, who Mya has aligned herself with, wanted to cremate her wearing a man's suit, dressed as a man with her dead name. For those that don't know, a dead name is the former name of a person. Silk didn't continue using her born first name or her parents' last name Little. She never went by the name Silk Little.

"Silk was a member of this church, while she was homeless and in need of employment. This church helped her to get a job. Her mother, Erica, refused to take her to the interview because Silk wasn't dressed like a man. Silk was heartbroken. Not because of the job, but because Titan Industries' own Erica Little, rejected Silk for being who she was. Silk then returned to sex work, began using narcotics, became homeless again, and soon after was murdered. Erica and her husband, Sedrick Little, wanted to cremate Silk, without notifying anyone. The owner of the funeral home around the corner from here, Allen Bradley, remembered Silk from high school and offered to give her a funeral for free just to give her some final respect. Erica Little chose to still make it a private viewing with only a very select number of people being present."

"Why are you bringing all that up now?" Mya asks rolling her eyes.

"Because that happened in this district. In the Old Market Place. If you're going to represent this district, you better know the history. You better know the people. You better know the struggle. We will listen and try our best to support yours, and those of the people in the Arts District, but that love has to go both ways," Hakeem responds.

"What about the people of Duke Hill? What about their needs? Things got so bad, they separated themselves from Ridgely Square. At least I have tried to patch that relationship up," Mya yells as members of the audience roll their eyes. I notice as Hakeem postures himself in a less imposing way. I've seen him act this way when we've had disagreements, when he wants to be heard but not come off as angry.

"Mya, I'm not attacking you, and if it appears that way, my apologies. We the people of Ridgely Square have been overlooked by the same people that we elected to look out for us. I truly admire all of the work you've done in the Arts District. It is impressive. The advocacy you've done at the state level is impressive as well. The issue is, those things you fought for did not reflect us. If you want our support, what is your agenda to support us?" Hakeem asks as Mya stands at the front of the church frozen. The silence in the chapel makes both sides tense, though all eyes are on Mya.

"I created the Justice 4 All organization to help everyone that requires advocacy, regardless of race, religion, sexual orientation or problem. I fought for Tyrone Clinton the same way I fought for Silk and Edward Carter. The 10th Bank was created with the help of local leaders to help combat gentrification. We don't get the support of the Flamingo Club on this side of the district, we would love to have it. What we have received is Titan Industries purchasing homes and creating economic barriers to the people that have called this community home for decades."

"Are you fighting to stop the murders of sex workers? Are you fighting to stop the Action Figure Killer? Are you fighting to bring the murderer of Jada Austin to justice?" Mya asks, appearing to hold back tears.

I am overcome with guilt, thinking about how hard this debate has to be on Mya, and the grief she has gone through. My knees began to shake as I feel a sudden need to get fresh air. I stand up and walk out of the worship area of the church and into the hallway, where the church announcements board, a table with pamphlets and the bathrooms are. Standing by the announcements board, looking at the pictures of deceased church members is Erica Little.

"I was too hard on Simon, I know that," Erica Little says, glancing at a picture of my grandmother, Pastor Donald and his wife Michelle Avery. In the picture they were in their early 30s and appeared very happy. One of the few pictures where I saw my grandmother smile. "I wanted the best for my son. I wanted the best for him and Sabrina. Sedrick and I did so much to build and continue our parents' legacy. We ran a small airline and hotels. We lost sight of things until Sabrina died. We wanted to have an image. What's crazy is, we tried to pour everything into Simon, and Simon never really recovered. He watched his sister die, running across a street to him. It was a crazy day. Simon was playing football or soccer, and the team lost. Sabrina was in a pageant, and she lost the competition. I was hard on her."

"What are you talking about? Why are you telling me this, and why now?" I ask Erica as her back is towards me looking at the picture.

"My mom and I didn't get along. It was always business, pageants, and finding a man that could grow the family company. They arranged the marriage of Sedrick and me. I'm saying this because I saw your mother's interaction with you," Erica says as my stomach drops. I think, maybe I should go back into the debate and get away from this lady.

"Your mother is cut throat. I listened to her talk as I drove her back to the inn. I did some research and learned that she doesn't own the house. It was left to you by Florence Simms, as it was willed to her. Neither Florence Simms's siblings nor any other family members have a claim to that house. While I would love to purchase your property for Titan Industries, I'm in the business of doing things the right way."

"Thanks, I already knew that," I state as I begin to walk back into the worship hall to watch the debate. Erica firmly grabs my forearm to stop me.

"I messed up with Simon. I didn't really understand or accept his life as a cross dresser," Erica says as I stop her from talking.

"Her name was Silk and she preferred to be referred to as she or her. She wasn't a cross dresser. She was a transwoman. Why can't you provide her with a little bit of respect? She was your child," I say, frustrated with Erica.

"Simon and Sabrina were twins, like your two oldest kids. Sabrina was in beauty pageants like I was as a child. All the way up to young adulthood. I even won Ms. Maryland. I was the first African American woman to win the tiara. Along with a traumatic situation that affected me for several decades, thanks to the pageant judges, I also was bestowed tons of confidence. I was respected, not just for my looks, but my brains and the power my parents had."

"I don't get it. Why do you continue to mock and disrespect Silk's legacy?" I ask.

"Because she wasn't a real woman. My son was mentally ill. He believed that Sabrina was living inside of him after she was killed by the hit and run. No matter how much I spent on psych drugs, and the thousands I dumped into therapy, he kept up with the psychosis. Why? Because society kept telling him his mental disorder was ok, it was his identity," Erica says, turning towards me with tears in her eyes.

"What if she had both? What if she was mentally ill, dealing with depression but also a transwoman? Would that be so bad? I mean you're backing somebody who is supporting that community. Does that mean anything to you?"

"Money. Growing this company. Getting trash like the Alphas and the Cabal off the streets. That's what means something to me now. I lost both my children and I'm losing my husband, thanks to Ridgely Square. You lost one of yours thanks to this place. Move out of here. Be a better parent to your children than I was to mine. It's not worth it for you to stay here. Find somewhere better. Somewhere with bigger yard space, better schools, less taxes, less crime. Somewhere where your kids can grow up and live a life you can be proud of," Erica says as she pulls a tissue out of her purse to clean her face.

"I'm not selling my house, Erica," I say, not buying her emotional behavior. Erica briefly smiles before the tone in her voice changes from sullen to upbeat.

"It was worth a shot. By the way, thank you for killing your father. It saved me a lot of time, going back and forth to court to talk about Simon, and learning about his lifestyle," Erica says, walking out of the glass doors of the church onto the cement steps. I feel so confused by her behavior. Why is she like this?

"I can't stand her," I hear a voice say out loud. I think for a moment it is Bell until I notice Jamar walking out of the bathroom, wiping his hands with a paper towel.

Chapter 9

That evening, Hakeem, Jamar, and I sit together in my living room to watch a televised interview with Anna Cartwright and the former police commissioner, Alex Tillman. Desha is seated at the kitchen table drawing one of her comic books as RJ and Trinity fuss about what they want to watch on their tablet. Darrin is outside with his friends.

"Commissioner, what can you tell me about the growing number of murders in the city? Specifically in the Ridgely Square community?" Anna Cartwright asks as Jamar and Hakeem watch closely from the couch.

Alex Tillman appears to be in a relaxed state. He seems to be happier since working with Agent Parker and Detective Murphy than he did as the police chief. He used to be so tense at all his press conferences.

"As you know, Ms. Cartwright, there's an ongoing investigation with the Alphas and the Narcotics and Firearms Task Force. That being said, I believe the majority of the murders happening in this city are being committed by the same people. The Alphas are killing people associated with the sex trafficking investigation. The murders are also related to the turf war between the Alphas and the Cabal," Alex Tillman answers.

"What do you think of the Action Figure Killer, also known as AFK? Is he related to the Alphas? Do the FBI or local law enforcement have any leads on who he is?" Anna asks as Alex Tillman briefly smiles.

"We believe that the Action Figure Killer, or Action Figure Killers, might be hitmen for the Alphas; they could also be members of the Cabal. So far, AFK has killed informants and associates of the Alphas that have been in contact with investigators," Alex answers.

"AFK has also killed the district attorney, Jada Austin," Anna interjects.

"This is true, and as he stated in the note he left, she was suppressing evidence for her own professional career," Alex quickly responds.

"Does the FBI have any idea who he is?" Anna Cartwright asks.

"We have leads, but no solid evidence. The FBI and our local investigation unit are doing everything possible to catch AFK. All we do know for sure is that AFK leaves a child's toy at the scene of the crime," Alex Tillman says with a slight smirk on his face.

"Thank you, Commissioner. Can you tell us more about the Alphas?" Anna asks as Alex Tillman sits back in his chair, assuming a more relaxed position.

"The Alphas are a nationwide gang, that originated in Baltimore City. They are known for trafficking drugs, such as opioids, marijuana and cocaine. They have also been involved in sex trafficking nationwide. During the time of Marshawn Bell's court case, he and Jada Austin made a deal with the judge and the FBI to provide more information about the sex trafficking. This came to light with the help of your friend, Gina Simms," Alex answers as Anna nods her head.

"Since working the investigation, have you spoken to Gina Simms?" Anna asks. Alex shakes his head no.

"Sadly, the FBI has limited my role in the investigation to just looking over the evidence and working with a few agents. This is just because of my familiarity with the Alphas," Alex answers.

"And the Alphas also murdered one of your officers a few years ago, correct?" Anna asks. Immediately Alex changes his posture.

"Yes, Edward Carter. He was a local football coach and an all-around great guy. I saw him as one of my sons. I was there the day he was murdered. I was also the person that returned fire, killing the two gang members. One of the worst memories of my life. Not for killing the Alphas but because they killed a person I loved as a son. I also loved Bell as a son, which led to sleepless nights when I learned in court that he put the hit out on Edward Carter," Alex says, looking down at his trembling hands.

"You mentioned loving them as your own children; do you have any children, Commissioner?" Anna asks, leaning her head forward. A new expression rushes over Alex Tillman's face. It's anger. It appears that he tries to hide it, but it is very visible.

"I had a son. His name was John. I didn't want to name him Alex Junior because I wanted him to have his own identity. Not to get too caught up in the story, but my father and my grandfather were both police officers. They were my motivation for being a police officer. Being a police officer is all I wanted to be growing up and all I cared about. It cost me my marriage, but I was able to keep John in the divorce. John was all set to go into the police academy, to become a cadet after high school. He and his friends went on a camping and kayaking trip in Tennessee, but an early-released convict killed my son. My only child," Alex Tillman says as his face turns red and his hands begin to shake again.

"I'm so sorry that you had to endure that. As you know, I was once the lead prosecutor in Tennessee. I wish I was there at that time to convict that person who brought you so much pain, that no parent should go through," Anna states as a breaking news ticker pops up on the screen.

"Actually, we have to pivot for a second, Commissioner Tillman, my apologies. We have learned that the body of the former Baltimore City Councilman, Dawson, was found moments ago. He was found murdered, and police have confirmed that he was a victim of AFK," Anna states with a look of shock on her face.

Inside the living room, Jamar, Hakeem and I look at each other as Anna continues to speak about the discovery of the former city councilman.

"Was Councilman Dawson tied to the sex trafficking case?" Hakeem asks as Jamar and I motion that we are not sure.

"He did resign pretty quickly. I mean, there's the 2020 election next year. He could have ridden this term out and not run for re-election next year. It must have been something, right?" Jamar asks as Desha walks in the room with another newly-drawn comic book to show him.

As I turn up the volume on the TV, Darrin walks into the house with a hoodie and sweatpants on. He glances at the TV screen, then at us before running upstairs.

"What's up with him?" Jamar asks, looking at me.

"I don't know. He's been hanging with this group of kids lately. I'm going to talk to him about it," Tiffany mentions as Jamar leans back in the chair.

"Maybe Hakeem should talk to him. Hear me out, with all the gang stuff, and how easy it is to fall into the life here, it would be good for a black man to talk to another black man," Jamar responds as Darrin runs back down the stairs with a different hoodie on.

"It's nothing going on. Y'all can chill. Go run your bank or whatever. I'm just doing what I have to do to keep us safe," Darrin says before storming out the house.

"Teenagers," I say dismissively.

"You don't really believe that, right?" Bell says in my ear. "He keeps going out the house at random times. He was hanging out with Cabal members at the playground the other day. He mentioned doing what he has to do to keep us safe. You might not want to hear this but he could be AFK."

Chapter 10

The next day, Paul and the gentleman that accompanied him to the church during the community meeting, come into my restaurant to speak with Hakeem and me. The breakfast rush has just slowed down and several tables are open. I really don't want to talk to Paul and feel uncomfortable around his friend who displayed a gun during our last meeting.

"Dr. Andrews and Ms. Tiffany Gibbons, my goal is to keep Ridgely Square the same or better than it was. The Flamingo Club has invested a lot of capital into the upkeep of the Arts District. Titan has done a lot to take over all of Ridgely Square and make it into something else. I would like to use my financial capital to help with the 10th Bank's mission and vision," Paul says as his partner stands bchind him to his right. His hair is short but curly. His eyes are light brown, and he is very articulate.

"I'm not sure what you're looking for," Hakeem states as Paul looks around the dining room area of the restaurant.

"This restaurant and market are just the beginning, am I correct? As large as the Market Place is, all these stores can open and flourish. What if I can help provide the capital to your bank to fulfill that mission? Pastor Donald Avery wanted something like that with a substance abuse treatment center, a counseling center, a shelter and a restaurant for your grandmother," Paul continues.

"Yes, Pastor Avery had the vision to open those places near the church," Hakeem interjects as Paul nods in agreement.

"I think it would be a great idea for us to work together," Paul continues. "I have a history of philanthropy in this community that includes giving school supplies, food, paying rent, and purchasing clothes for many of the people in need that live on the School Side, and the Ridgely Homes area. Of course we can go further and do greater things, together."

"But not all of the money that is provided to help the community is from the revenue you've earned from your lounge or your club, am I correct?" Hakeem asks as Paul looks on without an expression.

"I'm not going to sit here and lie to you. You both know my role with the Alphas. You both are also familiar with the investigation, and thanks to Gina Simms, my life has been difficult. That does not mean that business hasn't been good. My clubs have been making good money, but I need somewhere to dispose of the other income. The FBI is probing through my finances right now and asking a lot of questions. That being said, the 10th Bank would be perfect. You guys fulfill your mission, and I have somewhere to launder my money. Worst case scenario, you deny everything," Hakeem answers as I roll my eyes. I feel sick to my stomach, knowing what this man has done to young girls.

"This investigation that the FBI is conducting, is more so about the sex trafficking than the drugs, am I correct?" Hakeem asks.

"The FBI is investigating a sex trafficking ring," Paul answers. "I know your aunt, Gina Simms, believed that the Alphas were involved. Hopefully this will all be cleared up."

"I'm going to say no to the idea of a partnership. Respectfully, the 10th Bank cannot afford to be wrapped up in the sex trafficking investigation," Hakeem states as I nod in agreement.

"But you would be ok with the drug trafficking?" Paul asks as his accomplice reaches to his side pulling out the handle of a gun. As he was about to tug on the pistol, Alex

Tillman walks into the restaurant and is seated at a booth adjacent to us.

"We would prefer not to have any illegal money funnel through our banking institution," I state as Alex makes eye contact with me. Paul's associate takes his hand off the handle of the firearm and glances at Alex Tillman.

"There are preachers in Ridgely Square that are glad to take this money. There are families happy to take my generosity. But you all, a black owned bank that's supposed to be all about bettering the community says no? This is amazing. You're telling me no, even with Tiffany's mediocre looks, steady weight gain and impending high blood pressure. I commend you, to be honest. I want you to think it over, and I'll come back," Paul says as he and his associate leave the restaurant. Moments later Alex Tillman walks over to the table where Hakeem and I are sitting and he joined us uninvited.

"Interesting company you're keeping these days, Ms. Gibbons," Alex Tillman says as the waiter brings him a cup of coffee and a sandwich. "I never took you for one to participate in gang activity, especially after everything you endured a couple years ago."

"I'm not," I answer in fear of Alex Tillman. I was there that night he killed Marshawn Bell.

"Yes, you were," I hear Bell whisper into my ear.

"How well do you know Paul Douglass and his associate Roland Wise?" Alex Tillman asks after taking a bite out of his smoked prime rib, avocado, egg and cheese sandwich. I look on, eager to see his expression after the first bite because that is one of my signature sandwiches at the restaurant. I notice his closed eyes and smile of approval while chewing.

"We don't know him at all. Other than the fact that he wants to partner with our bank. We told him no," I answer. "We don't know who Roland Wise is."

"Roland is a former United States Marine. He worked in special forces, off the books missions. He went into countries, took out high profile targets and got out. He was dishonorably discharged after crippling a captain for giving him post orders to serve for Marine One in 2005 for President George W. Bush. He thought it was an insult because of the President going AWOL during his time in the military. Years later Roland killed three of his babies' mothers' partners. Was incarcerated and then released after divulging information about a correctional officer's participation in illegal activities," Alex mentions as the restaurant appears to go quiet.

"Roland was rumored to have smuggled people from Nicaragua, Ghana, Ecuador, Venezuela and Columbia into the United States without detection. He made money by providing fake visas and new lives for many of these people. He also found himself on Paul's radar and became his top lieutenant. While I was the police chief I was watching him for a few murders of immigrant sex workers, but the former mayor, Asia Wall, was caught up in a scandal that ruined my whole case. Since then, Roland Wise has been a ghost." Alex takes a sip of his coffee.

"Great, and that guy was inside of my restaurant," I say with my heart beating out of my chest.

"Do you think he's the Action Figure Killer?" Hakeem asks as Alex chuckles and says no.

"We don't know who AFK is. That being said, I seriously doubt that Roland Wise is AFK. Off the record, I don't think AFK is associated with the Alphas or the Cabal," Alex says as he goes back to chewing his sandwich.

"What should we do about Roland and Paul?" I ask as Hakeem asks a waiter for a cup of sweet tea.

"You two are good people. Stay away from Paul, first and foremost. The Alphas are cleaning house, which is bad news for anybody associated with them. Secondly, keep making these sandwiches. This is really good, Ms. Gibbons," Alex says as he continues to eat his sandwich.

Chapter 11

A few days later, Hakeem, Jamar and I are sitting inside one of the classrooms at the community center discussing the upcoming election. Jamar is sitting on the metal desk that has a wooden top. The desk is covered with papers, folders and boxes of board games. The room smells like fresh paint and has several random items inside of it, including tables with desks attached to them, paint cans, boxes with tables and chairs, and clothing racks filled with men's and women's dress clothes.

"Bro, I'm just saying, do you really think that now is the best time to run for public office? We have everything going on with the bank, and it's working. This is a weird side step, and I don't think it's necessary for our success," Jamar says to Hakeem who is sitting on top of one of the chair-connected desks.

"This is a perfect move," Hakeem responds. "Think about it, we have the bank, and we start working in City Hall. We can stop Titan Industries and make this whole district into something beautiful."

"We need to finish what we started here in Ridgely Square first. I think you running for office is great, but I can't run this bank without you," Jamar continues. "Not with my record. I would get shredded. It would really bring our credibility into question. Tiffany has been doing a great job, but she would be limited to her dedication to the bank while running her restaurant and the market. Clair from Nubian Media has only committed to helping with funding and some guidance. Allen Bradley is running the funeral home, he's limited. It has to be you."

"This is a once in a life time opportunity," Hakeem counters as I shake my head in disagreement.

"No Hakeem, it's not," I state to his surprise. "You have a long life ahead of you. A great long life. So far you have successfully partnered with the Baltimore City Police Department to improve the community's relationship, you have brought justice for families like the Lyles-Bey family, and helped people in great need. Together with this bank you have helped so many residents and up and coming business owners. If you win this seat, will you run for re-election?"

"Yes, of course, the city-wide election is in 2020," Hakeem answers.

"If you win that one, then what?" I ask.

"I keep fighting against gentrification, redlining, racial injustice, lowering the crime rate, improving home ownership for African Americans, and improving the school system," Hakeem answers as Jamar turns completely towards him.

"Why can't you do that through the 10th Bank?" Jamar asks as he leans forward. "You have all the gifts to do this, and hell, if we can't help you within the next 4 to 5 years, run in 2024 on that platform. At least your resume will show that you've tried to do this through an organization. You can pat yourself on the back for what worked, and fight harder for what didn't. But this community needs you now with the bank."

"You two don't get it," Hakeem says, trying to balance himself on the little desk. "Mya Rodriguez's agenda is aligned with Titan Industries. It will crush us in the long run. We can't afford to let that happen. In case everyone in here has forgotten, Titan Industries is the real enemy. Not the Alphas, not NAFA, not Paul Douglass and not AFK, it's Titan Industries."

"Erica is going to sabotage Titan Industries again," I say as Jamar agrees. "Mya, doesn't even realize that Erica isn't an ally to her people, the LGBTQ. It's just a matter of time before Erica Little puts her foot in her mouth again, like she did at Pastor Avery's wake."

"What are you talking about?" Jamar inquires.

"Four years ago, Silk's viewing was held at the same time as Pastor Avery's viewing. At the same funeral home and everything. Erica and her husband, Sedrick Little, tried to have a private viewing because they were ashamed that Silk was a transwoman. To this day, Erica calls Silk by her born name, and calls Silk by male pronouns," I answer.

"When was the last time you heard her do this?" Hakeem inquires, standing up and walking around the room.

"A couple days ago, at the debate," I answer, as all of our phones begin to buzz at the same time. I pull out my phone to read a report, that says in bold letters that the Police Commissioner Junior Dawson was murdered, and it is a confirmed AFK shooting.

The report says that AFK left the Baltimore City Police Department a note stating that Junior Dawson tipped off his father, Councilman Dawson, about the FBI investigation. The note also states that Councilman Dawson was involved in paying for sex workers that were involved with the Alphas, many of whom were underaged girls.

In addition to tipping off his father, Junior Dawson tipped off several lawyers, judges, police officers and citizens that they were listed on one of the USB drives now in the custody of the FBI. In addition to the names of known associates and customers listed on the USB drives, it states that the recently murdered State's Attorney Jada Austin withheld evidence about the deceased NAFA Sargent Marshawn Bell to use as leverage for his freedom.

AFK said in his note that Jada Austin's abuse of power led to the current investigation conducted by the FBI but has cost several lives. AFK vowed in his letter not to harm innocent hard working people, but swore to bring judgment to the individuals involved in the sex trafficking ring and drug trade. AFK also denied being affiliated in any way with the Alphas or the Cabal.

Chapter 12

Later that afternoon, Paul and Roland are seated at a booth in my restaurant with Jamar and me. Paul comes prepared with several folders filled with documents, along with a tablet that has a PowerPoint presentation. In no way, shape or form am I interested in looking at that PowerPoint presentation.

"Tiffy, we are very serious about doing business with you," Paul states, being very persistent. If he wasn't so easy on the eyes, I would have asked him to leave 30 minutes ago. That, and the fact that I am genuinely afraid of Roland Wise. I really wish Hakeem was present, but he wants to distance himself from Roland and Paul due to the election.

"We respect everything that you all have been doing," Paul continues. "That being said, we have shown how successful we can be. Not one person during the last holiday season had to go without food and plenty of gifts, thanks to us. Not one church had to struggle financially, thanks to us. We have the money, let us place it in your institution. It's an easy win."

"We're not going to do business with you, Paul. You have done a lot for this community, no doubt about that, but when this investigation is finished, where does that leave this restaurant or the bank?" Jamar asks. "This community deserves to have a part in something with dignity. Not more of the same thing that has crippled it."

"I get it, you don't want to get killed by AFK. I totally don't blame you. He's killing politicians, drug dealers, prostitutes and everyone in between. We have something for him," Paul says, pointing at Roland Wise.

"We don't care about that. All of that is unnecessary for us," Jamar rebuts. "AFK isn't after us. The kids in my community center wear AFK shirts. If you look around this restaurant, you'll see people here with shirts on that say AFK. He's reduced crime in this district, and people love him for it. We don't want the crime element involved in our bank. We don't want the drug or the sex trafficking money. Like I said, the people of Ridgely Square deserve more."

"Aren't you a convicted felon?" Paul asks. Jamar nods his head to confirm.

"I am. And I left that part of my life behind, as you know. I use my life story as a testimony for young men and women to strive to be more than I was," Jamar answers. "Look at my brother. He's running for public office, he's the pastor of a church, he's running a bank and he's about to get married. That's the example we are trying to push at the 10th Bank. Look at Tiffany, a single mom of four, a college graduate and a business owner."

"Everybody doesn't have what Tiffany has," Paul states. My stomach drops. I think really hard about whether Paul could possibly know about the money I accepted from Marshawn Bell. There's no way he could know. The only person that knows is Sasha, and she won't tell nobody.

"What do I have?" I ask in fear of what he might say.

"Aside from a good looking ass, a decent face and body?" Paul says as if that was a compliment. "You have a home you inherited from your grandmother and money left over from her will that enabled you to open this restaurant."

I exhale, so glad that is all he knows.

"You know how many people I give money to because their child was murdered or their mother died of whatever? Funerals are expensive. I help provide a safety net. I might as well start an insurance company," Paul jokes.

"Why can't you just open another night club, or another strip club?" I ask. Paul winks at me.

"You want to shake that ass at my club, huh? Being in the kitchen must have gotten hard for you," Paul responds. "I mentioned this to you before, that level of revenue would bring too much attention to my company. The Federal Bureau of Investigation isn't a group of dumb people. I'm trying to get off their radar. You guys aren't on it. I get that you're protecting Hakeem, and I'm going to stay far away from his campaign, but I need to get my money into your bank. I'm not taking no for an answer."

"The answer is no," Jamar says, pushing the folders back to Paul. "We are not going to have our business tied up with you and what you have going on. Can't you take this to the Italians in Duke Hill or someone in the Arts District?"

"No," Paul answers quickly. "Years ago, I provided support for your community resource center to have school supplies, Jamar. I didn't think twice about it. I also put you up in a room for rent when you came home from prison. Do you remember when you were exiled from your family and nobody from the same mosque you minister at now could help you with housing? I did it and didn't think twice about it. I was happy to help. I felt like I was in a position to help and you were my responsibility to help.

My brother's keeper. Now the shoe is on the other foot, and you're telling me no."

"It's not the same, Paul, and you know it. This could jeopardize so much. Employees, freedom, other companies. You understand that, right?" Jamar asks as Paul and Roland exit the booth and walk away, leaving the folders and several papers scattered on the table.

"I don't think this is going to end pretty," Jamar says, looking at some of the documents left on the table.

"Do you think we did the right thing? I mean meeting with Paul without Hakeem. Was that the right thing to do?" I ask. I know we both agreed that keeping Hakeem far away from this was the best thing, but Paul seemed to take the rejection personally.

"Why doesn't he take his business to the Arts District or to Duke Hill? Why not take his business to Titan Industries or the Flamingo Club? He could get away with it, with the money and the connections they have there. Why harass us?" I ask as Hakeem walks into the restaurant and sits across from Jamar and me.

"This campaign is a nightmare," Hakeem states, completely unaware of the meeting that took place until he glances at one of the documents on the table. "What did I miss?"

"Well, you missed Paul and his bulldog, Roland leaving out of here disappointed. Of course he took the rejection personally," I state as Jamar tries to smile. He is visibly upset because of what transpired between him and Paul.

"What's going on with you, bro?" Jamar says, attempting to cheer himself up.

"Mya has been campaigning all over the district. She has placed billboards everywhere. She has the financial backing of the Flamingo Club and Titan Industries, and it shows. You can't even walk into a liquor store without seeing her flier. I'm surprised she hasn't put one up in here yet," Hakeem jokes, looking at the windows of the restaurant.

"I have to leave real quick, there was a bad fight with a few of the kids at the community center. Hakeem, you want me to come by your house or Tiffany's house later?" Jamar questions as he looks down at his phone at a text message. He then scoots out of the booth and walks toward the door.

"We definitely need to recap and talk about this. Let's meet at my house," Hakeem says to Jamar, pointing at the folders on the table. He then turns to Tiffany. "I promise after this election is over, we're going to spend more time together and get to work planning the wedding."

"You sure this isn't too much? We can always slow down," I say. Hakeem responds by shaking his head no, but before Hakeem can open his mouth to speak, we hear several gunshots coming from outside the restaurant.

Several people in the restaurant begin to panic, so I try to calm them. Darrin runs inside of the restaurant towards Hakeem and me with panic, fear, and concern in his eyes.

"You, you need to come with me now," he says, running back towards the door. Hakeem and I follow him to the end of the block of boarded-up stores, and in the midst of a lot of litter, Jamar lies lifeless on the ground on his side. Hakeem yells loudly in anger and grief as I notice a Spiderman toy next to his body.

"I'm going to kill him," Hakeem says, kneeling on the ground, sobbing and holding his brother's head. "I'm going to kill AFK."

"We have a problem," I hear Bell whisper into my ear.

"What's the problem?" I ask out loud as Hakeem glances back at me with his eye burning in anger and sadness. He is unsure who I'm speaking with. I know Bell is dead and this version of him is an auditory hallucination, but the voices in my head of Marshawn Bell, my grandmother, my cousin Tina and sometimes my daughter Kenya are something I have never shared with Hakeem. I really try to keep these voices under wraps and hidden. They used to speak to me in the basement of my grandmother's house, but after I stopped my father, Bell and my grandmother have become more invasive in my everyday life.

"We don't know who AFK is," Bell continues, as Hakeem turns his attention back to his brother. Multiple police cars and an ambulance approach the area where we are, and a crowd of spectators grow and stand in the distance.

"Not only do we not know who AFK is, we don't know if he'll be back," Bell continues. I begin to feel fearful of my surroundings. "AFK could be anybody, including Paul, Roland or—"

"Don't say it!" I scream out loud. Hakeem glances back towards me.

"Why was Darrin here? Why was he in this area at the same time of the murder? Where has he been going? We need to know… is Darrin AFK?" Bell asks repeatedly in my mind as I sit down next to Hakeem, with my head between my knees and my arms holding my legs. I feel my knees shake uncontrollably as the tears begin to fall from my eyes.

"How did I miss the signs?" I ask out loud.

"What signs?" Hakeem asks as officers walk towards us.

"AFK must have seen us at dinner with Paul and figured we were doing business with him," I say aloud.

"I don't care. He killed my brother. Jamar didn't do nothing to nobody," Hakeem says angrily at me, as a police officer attempts to help me up.

Chapter 13

Some time went by, not sure if it was 30 minutes, not sure if it was 2 hours, but Darrin, Hakeem and I are sitting inside of my manager's office at the restaurant with Alex Tillman, Detective Murphy and Agent Parker. Everything seems to be hazy. We give several accounts of what we know to multiple officers, who threaten to take my son Darrin away in handcuffs as a suspect, and at one point Hakeem is blamed for tampering with a crime scene for crying and cradling his brother.

The icing on the cake, though, is being told that we have to contact a funeral home and have them coordinate with the medical examiner's office to pick up Jamar's body. Hakeem explains Jamar's religious practices, and the importance of having him buried as soon as possible, but the officers are dismissive.

Detective Murphy and Agent Parker request to meet with Hakeem and me at the restaurant before we leave to talk to the other children at the house.

"Again, sorry about your loss," Agent Parker says in a low tone while looking at Hakeem, who is looking down at the floor. "I know you have gone through this with so many other officers, but can you tell us anything about what you heard or saw?"

"I just heard the gun shots. I was sitting in a booth, with my fiancée. I didn't know it was Jamar that was shot. Why would AFK shoot him?" Hakeem states looking down with a low tone.

"You said Roland Wise and Paul Douglass came here requesting to do business with y'all earlier, correct Ms. Gibbons?" Detective Murphy asks. I nod in agreement. "This goes back to my theory that Roland Wise is AFK."

"He's not AFK, he's a copycat killer, if anything, related to AFK," Alex Tillman states, very sure of himself.

"How do you know that?" Darrin asks, staring down Detective Murphy.

"There are details we have not informed the public," Detective Murphy responds, looking Darrin in the eye.

"Like what?" I ask, followed by Hakeem.

"As you know, the Action Figure Killer leaves a calling card at the scene of the crime. A child's toy. In the case of

Jamar, it was a Spiderman toy. That's not on brand with AFK's signature toy," Detective Murphy states.

"Are you saying AFK didn't kill my brother?" Hakeem questions, looking up to Detective Murphy still having a staring contest with my son.

"Not likely," Detective Murphy answers. "Can your son leave the room for a second. We're going to share some sensitive information, and I don't want this to get out to his friends. He knows who they are and what I'm talking about."

I shoot my eyes over to Darrin who quickly looks away from me and leaves out of the office, closing the door behind him.

"The Action Figure Killer is more than likely an African American male," Detective Murphy says. "The reason we feel that way is because of his ability to go and come in this community without standing out, or raising any suspicions. I felt like it was someone related very closely to this FBI investigation with the Alphas. The former commissioner is stating that all the evidence points in a different direction."

Alex Tillman turns towards me as I lean to the side in the office chair and says, "Yes, while I'm unsure of the race, I highly doubt this AFK person is on good terms with the Alphas. I also don't believe he is related to the Cabal. He is more of a vigilante than a gang member. I feel that way not only by how the murders were conducted but also his choice of calling card. A little green plastic Army man toy."

"That detail about the toy is how we know the copycat killer from the real AFK," Agent Parker states quickly. "That's why it's important that the detail about the type of toy it is does not leave this room."

"I wish it *was* Paul Douglass or Roland Wise," Detective Murray says. "We have been investigating them for years. I once had them until the former mayor, Asia Wall screwed the whole investigation with her illegal use of a wiretap."

"Was Asia Wall's murder considered an AFK killing?" Hakeem asks, leaning his head to the side and looking down at the floor.

"Not initially. But we recently went back over a lot of the evidence that was collected, and we found a picture with a little green Army man standing next to her head," Detective Murphy states.

"Ms. Gibbons, may I hold your phone to place our numbers in. In the event of an emergency, I want you to

call us as soon as possible," Alex Tillman says as I hand
him my phone.

Chapter 14

Later this evening Hakeem, the children and I gather together at the kitchen table discussing memories we shared with Jamar. It isn't an easy event, but necessary. We cried and we laughed about some of the stories.

Desha discusses how Jamar motivated her to follow her dream to enroll into art school. RJ and Trinity talk about their desire to play basketball and start a music production company. Darrin is very quiet, with rage and anger written all over his face. Every chance he can, he attempts to leave the house to go outside with his friends, but I stop him.

Unexpectedly we hear the doorbell, which creates tense fear and anxiety. I can feel my heart pounding as Hakeem gets up from the table, followed by Darrin. When I attempt to pull Darrin back, he drags me towards the door with him and Hakeem.

Hakeem answers the door, and to his surprise, he finds Mya standing on the other side, dressed in jeans and a zipped up hoodie. There is heavy rain falling that we failed to notice while in the kitchen.

"Hey Dr. Andrews, I went by your house earlier and didn't get an answer, so I figured you were here. I wanted to give my condolences," Mya says as she hands him a large bag with boxes of food inside.

"I know it's late," she continues, "I just wanted to make sure you and the family had something to eat."

"Thank you, Ms. Rodriguez," Hakeem says in a low tone, accepting the bag from her.

"I'm suspending my campaign," Mya says as Hakeem turns his back to go in the house. "It's not right to run against a person who's grieving."

"You don't have to do that," Hakeem says, as he turns back around to face her. "You continued to campaign against me when Jada Austin was murdered."

"I had to. Nobody knew that we were a couple but her and me. Of course I told Tiffany, who was with me the night they found her," Mya counters.

"No, you don't have to suspend your campaign," Hakeem remarks. "I'm withdrawing my name from the election."

"No, don't do that. Grieve and give yourself time to heal. Don't get out of the election. Don't let the Alphas or

AFK beat you. This district loves and respects you," I say as he places his arm around me in an embrace.

"It's ok," Hakeem says to me in a low tone.

"Dr. Andrews, with all due respect, I would like you to reconsider this. I respect you too much to see you turn down an office you might win by a landslide," Mya says, and I agree.

"Can we meet at a later date to discuss my concerns? I think we can gain middle ground with the district. I know you have your position with Titan, and I have mine with 10th Bank. Somewhere in the middle is a fair balance. That being said, I'm out of this bid for office," Hakeem mentions before turning back to go inside with the food.

"Again, I'm so sorry for your loss, Dr. Andrews. I just don't know how AFK was able to do that to your brother and Anna Cartwright within the same timeframe," Mya says. As she's about to walk down the stairs I grab her elbow to stop her.

"What did you just say?" I ask, in shock at the news she just delivers.

"People in the community say that AFK killed Jamar. About a half hour before that shooting, Anna Cartwright was stabbed multiple times and shot in her car. There was a wreath with little toys attached to it on her passenger seat with a note, stating that she was a crooked prosecutor and that AFK is on a quest for justice," Mya says, seemingly puzzled that we didn't know.

After telling Mya goodnight, Hakeem and I make sure the kids are in bed. Hakeem goes to sleep on the recliner in the living room as the news plays; I fall asleep with RJ in my bed.

Sometime after 2:00 a.m. there is a loud bang, and the smoke detectors begin to sound. I jump up and hear Hakeem running up the stairs. There is heavy heat and flames coming from Trinity's room. Hakeem grabs her and rushes her downstairs. I run into Desha's room to wake her, as Darrin runs out of his room looking for RJ, who is still asleep, and he carries him downstairs.

My mind is filled with panic, as Hakeem goes to open the door. Darrin stops Hakeem from going outside first and he runs out with a small handgun in his hand looking up and down the sidewalk.

I am totally caught off guard when I see the firearm in my son's hand. Hakeem brings Trinity out first, and I see she is burned pretty badly on her right side. RJ and Desha walk out closely behind Hakeem. Looking at the front of our house I see flames shooting out from one of the top floor windows.

I notice Roland running across the street. He stops for a brief moment and points towards a Batman toy laying just inside my yard.

"You should have taken the deal," Roland screams as he runs off in the opposite direction of Darrin. Hearing Roland's voice, Darrin and Hakeem turn around to chase him, but Roland is quickly out of sight.

"Where did you get that gun from?" I scream at Darrin.

"Why? You need to chill. This right here probably is the only thing keeping us alive tonight," Darrin screams back.

"Give it to me!" I scream at him, and I reach towards his hand. Darrin snatches his hand back, but keeps the gun pointed away from me and his siblings.

"No, I have to keep us safe," Darrin screams as the sound of sirens can be heard. The dark sky is now interrupted by oncoming red lights from the fire trucks, and blue lights from police cars.

"You can't, you're still a child," I say as I snatch the gun and placed it in my pants pocket. Hakeem hands me a jacket to cover up with.

"I can't afford for you to go to prison for being dumb. Do you understand me? Do you know Sasha's son was murdered by police for having a gun?" I scream as Darrin attempts to walk off, but stops when he sees Trinity crying in fear and pain.

Chapter 15

A few hours later Hakeem, the children and I are at the West Baltimore Hospital Burn Unit. In the family meeting room, Detective Murphy and Agent Parker stand near the door as we sit near a table. There are no windows in the room, just a lot of full bookshelves, a large boardroom table, and a coffee machine.

RJ and Desha are visibly shaken by the fire. Darrin's angry gaze never breaks from my face. Hakeem's face is a mixture of anger, exhaustion and sadness. I too have growing anger inside of me for multiple reasons. The first reason is that my oldest son had a gun and was walking around the street with it like he was in the wild west. The second reason is that the only place we can afford to live is a house I inherited from my grandmother, which was just set on fire. We cannot afford another place to live and I refuse to move into Hakeem's house with my responsibilities. Which means I might be homeless again. The third reason is Jamar was just murdered hours ago.

With all of these feelings of anger swimming around in my head, I had to hide Darrin's gun in a trashcan in the emergency room. Anything could have gone wrong. Anything still could. Darrin's and my fingerprints are on that gun. Where did Darrin get that gun from? Did Jamar give him the gun, like he gave me one a couple years ago? Did he get it from one of his friends that he's been hanging out with? So many questions run through my mind as I try to look normal at Detective Murphy. What does looking normal look like?

"We just wanted to let you all know that we are searching for Roland Wise. He will be charged and brought to justice," Detective Murphy says in a matter of fact way.

"Can you think of anyone else who might be connected with the burning of your home?" Detective Murphy asks.

"Erica Little or my mother, Linda Gibbons, whatever officers associated with the NAFA case are still out there, and the Alphas," I answer, hoping I didn't leave anybody off the list.

"Do you think the fire-bombing has anything to do with AFK or the sex trafficking case with the Alphas?" Hakeem asks.

"With Roland Wise possibly being involved, I'm putting money on the Alphas. I don't believe he's AFK, but it appears that he's attempting to mimic the Action Figure Killer," Agent Parker answers.

"Your mother was here the whole night, Ms. Gibbons. She wouldn't have had any connection with the bombing of your house," Detective Murphy blurts out to my surprise.

"Why was she here?" I ask as Detective Murphy and Agent Parker send questioning looks to each other.

"We searched for her to make sure she was safe," Agent Parker starts. "We had a bad feeling that someone was targeting your family after Jamar Andrews was murdered, and your house was set on fire. We located your mother here at the hospital. It appears she had a massive heart attack and is being treated for organ failure."

"What?" I say, standing up in shock. "What room is she in? I have to see her!"

"Ms. Gibbons, I will have a nurse come meet with you about it immediately," Agent Parker states as Hakeem glances over at me.

"Tiffany, we need you here. Your kids are scared. We can see your mother soon, but let's make sure that Trinity is ok first," Hakeem states. I nod my head at Hakeem then look past him, as the look Detective Murphy is giving

Darrin catches my attention. I begin to stare back at him, wondering what his behavior is about.

"Why are you looking at my son like that?" I ask Detective Murphy.

"He started it," the detective says with a grin. He opens the door to leave the room.

"We'll get a nurse to talk to you about your mother. You both have my prayers, and I'm sorry for your loss, Dr. Andrews," Parker says.

Detective Murphy and Agent Parker walk out of the room as I notice Darrin's anger-fueled gaze aimed towards me.

"What?" I scream at Darrin as he appears to look through me.

"You took the gun from me," Darrin yells.

"Yes, I had to!" I respond.

"You need me, and I have to protect us," Darrin retorts. "Do you know I heard you and grandma talk all those times about what granddad did to you. She acted like you were lying, but we both know you told the truth."

"That's none of your business," I say to Darrin, trying to get him to stop talking around Hakeem and the others.

"It is, it started being my business that day when we were little and granddad beat you up, and did what he did to you in front of Desha and me," Darrin says to my surprise. They were so young then, 2 or 3 years old. How could he have known or remembered that?

"Then you add in all the men, in and out your life. The ones that hit you, beat on you, stole from you, beat on us. Do you remember all the times we had to move? It was my job to protect us. You said I was the oldest boy, and it was my job to be the man of the family. I was that," Darrin continued as TJ and Desha nodded in agreement.

"When grandad broke into the house, he was going to do something to you, or us. You stopped him. That should have been me. When grandad did what he did to Tina, I should have stopped him. When Bell kidnapped you from in front of the house, I should have stopped him. I don't want to live in should or would haves anymore. We can't afford it," Darrin says as Hakeem begins rubbing his right hand against his forehead in frustration and exhaustion.

"You and Hakeem are engaged; I'm happy for you. He's been more of a dad to us than my own dead ass daddy. Desha would agree our dad wasn't nothing when he was alive, so the closest person we ever had to a father figure, aside from Hakeem, was Mr. Keyon. But Mr. Keyon is dead, along with our younger sister, Kenya. I got to do my best to make sure that we don't lose any more family members," Darrin says as tears stream from his eyes.

"I can't lose any of y'all. Hakeem can leave tomorrow, if he wants to. He's not blood. You and us are all blood. I have to do what I have to do to keep us safe. You don't like it, but it's real," Darrin finishes before staring at me in silence.

"Are you selling drugs?" I ask. He shakes his head no. "Are you in a gang?"

"They my family. I only bang with them to protect us," Darrin answers in a deep and authoritative voice.

"You can't protect us, you're a child!" I scream back at him.

"I have been for years," Darrin responds and stands up with his fingers planted on the table. "When Aunt Gina started talking to the feds about the Alphas and NAFA, the community labeled us as snitches. They were going to burn our house down and kill us. I cleared our name and went with the Cabal for protection. Every Alpha that tried to kill any of us got dealt with by the Cabal. The police didn't do a damn thing to protect us. You know why?

Because y'all was telling on the police. You think they cared about you telling on the bad police and not the good police? They ain't give a damn, it was still police, Ma!"

"What's your role in the Cabal? If you not selling, you doing something," I say as Darrin rolls his eyes and tries to get from behind the table. The room is very tight to move around in.

"I'm a muscle. Basically an enforcer. I watch the block for the hustlers. If they need someone to get dealt with, I deal with them," Darrin says as I try to stop him from leaving the room.

"Where are you going?" I ask.

"I have to find my gun. Someone has to keep us safe. Mr. Jamar is dead, we can't afford to lose any other family members," Darrin says, snatching the door open to find Erica Little standing on the outside.

"What are you doing here?" I ask in a very annoyed tone as Erica applies a fake look of concern. Darrin stands next to me in an aggressive posture.

"Hi, Ms. Gibbons," Erica says in a chipper tone. Why is she here and so early in the morning?

"What do you want?" Darrin questions in a challenging tone.

"I went by your house after I got a call about the fire. It looks pretty rough and might cost a fortune in repairs. I don't want you to worry, I talked to my team at Titan Industries and we are ready to make you a very competitive offer for the property," Erica says, seemingly ecstatic.

"No!" I shout. "We have home insurance, the house is covered."

"Ms. Gibbons, I would like for you to think about all the scenarios. If this happened in the middle of the night, imagine what might happen during the day. There's always a next time. Don't you think these kids deserve to live in a better community?" Erica says as Darrin aggressively approaches her.

"Get out of here, and never come back. It would be in your best interest. Our house is not for sale," Darrin says in a low deep tone, rubbing his fist and cracking the knuckles on his right hand.

"I'm speaking to the homeowner," Erica says as Darrin appears to try to fight her. I stop him and slam the door on Erica.

"Don't do that," I say to Darrin. "She will sue us and take everything, do you understand that?"

"She only responds to one type of thing," Darrin says, annoyed.

"That's not how people operate in the real world," Hakeem says, finally looking up.

"That type of attitude will only get you killed in the long run, ask my brother. I used to focus on getting to the Promised Land, he would focus on what to do with the people in the Promised Land," Hakeem says, shaking his head in reflection of his brother.

"What happened to the people living in the Promised Land, in the Bible?" RJ asks.

"When they went around the walls of Jericho seven times, they blew the trumpets, went in and killed all the people that were living inside. Jamar always believed that we can't live in peace with the enemy. We have to slaughter the enemy in order to have peace," Hakeem says, looking at the wooden table.

"What are you saying?" I ask.

"Jamar could have been right. I'm not talking about slaughtering Erica Little, but we might have to figure out how to change our attack with Titan to get rid of them once and for all.

"I'm worried about him," Bell whispers into my ear as I glance at Hakeem and see rage and anger in his eyes.

Chapter 16

It's been a few days and Hakeem, Desha, RJ, Darrin and I are standing at Jamar's gravesite with members of his mosque and others from the community. It is a cloudy day, I constantly witness nimbus clouds gathering above, the wind is very high and we can feel the storm brewing. I also feel my melatonin levels rise, from having my child staying at a burn unit in the hospital, to having my home set on fire, to having my oldest son turn into a gun-toting gangster, to running a company. I need a break. Some sleep. In a way I feel jealous of all the resting souls in this cemetery. We feel sorry for them, but in all honesty, we're the ones that have to do all the work.

Erica Little stands a little ways behind me to my right side. I don't know why she's here, especially since she is the direct competition to the 10th Bank.

I watch as members of the community leave from the gravesite. I am dressed in the same black and gold dress I wore to my grandmother's funeral four years ago. Hakeem is dressed in a black suit, with a black button up shirt, a red and gold tie and red pocket square. He looks very sharp. If he wasn't my fiancé, I would have hit on him. I mean, hitting on the grieving good looking brother is like hitting on the best man at a wedding, right?

"That's sick, even for me," Bell whispers into my ear. I am careful not to respond out loud. I am fearful of what others will think or say. The co-founder of the 10th Bank and the Legacy of Florence owner was found speaking to herself and hearing voices. Not a good look.

"But he is good looking. It doesn't count, I guess. Seeing that you're about to marry him soon. Have you two picked a date yet?" Bell continues as I shake my head and try to look around at the guests that linger. I notice Paul walking towards the gravesite, and standing to Hakeem's right side.

"It's a shame that things have come to this," Paul says, looking down at the mound of fresh dirt that covers the body of Jamar.

Hakeem doesn't notice Paul at first, but as he makes eye contact, his fist clinches up and his posture changes into an aggressive stance.

"I'm glad that we have your attention now. I didn't want to have things go any further than where they have gone," Paul says as Hakeem attempts to punch him. I stand between Hakeem and Paul with the goal of stopping him.

"Don't do this, not here at least," I plead. "You know what you mean to this community," I say in a low tone to Hakeem as I hear Bell's voice yelling angry statements in my head.

"Does it even matter when people like him get to live and walk around freely?" Hakeem rebuts as Paul nods.

"It is very worth it, Dr. Andrews," Paul interjects. "I just wanted to do business with you all. Something that would make us all wealthy and successful."

"You burned my house down," I say in an angry tone. "My daughter is in the burn unit because of you!"

"That was AFK, Tiffany. By the way, you have the sexiest dimples I have ever seen. I see why you're engaged," Paul says in a condescending and arrogant tone.

"You know that wasn't AFK," Hakeem yells as others look on. Paul briefly flashes a gun at Hakeem and me before a smirk slides across his face.

"Sugar tits, can you tell the good reverend that no hard feelings are involved; it was all business. Plus, your house will be renovated. It was just some structural damage to the 2nd floor," Paul explains.

I feel angry and a sense of responsibility to Hakeem. I don't want Hakeem to lose his cool and get killed by Paul. At the same time, I want to kill Paul myself.

"You killed your own father, what's one more body," Bell jokes in my ear.

"Where is your buddy, Roland Wise?" Hakeem asks with bass in his voice.

"Check your tone, grimace," Paul says in a low tone. "I'd like to start doing business with you as soon as possible. For the sake of your kids, get on the same page and let's talk," Paul says as he makes eye contact with Darrin, standing at a distance.

Mya walks up behind Hakeem and me, startling us with an embrace. "Dr. Andrews, I don't want to leave without giving you and Tiffany my love. I'm so sorry this happened to your family."

"Thank you," Hakeem barely voices as he looks on in Paul's direction. He is clearly distracted as drops of rain fall from the sky.

"I was hoping to see some of your family. Your father, Bishop Andrews was an important member of this community and was connected to so many stakeholders," Mya says as Hakeem's attention turns towards her. The black Lincoln Town Car Paul enters slowly leaves the cemetery as Darrin studies the car.

"Yeah, my family didn't show up. I didn't expect them to. Not since my family alienated Jamar when he changed his religion to Islam," Hakeem says, still looking in the direction the car went. My feelings of anger change to fear, after thinking about what happened to Jamar and the house. Thoughts race through my mind. Will Paul return? What will Roland do next? Will they harm my children?

"Why? Why would your family alienate themselves from Jamar?" Mya asks. "He's done so much for the community."

"The black community is an interesting group. We forgive police shootings of unarmed black people, we forgive child molesters, we turn a blind eye to substance abuse and mental illness. With all that said, we can't forgive a family member for thinking for themself."

"Facts," I blurt out as I search for Darrin. He appears to have left the cemetery. Where did he go? Did Paul get him? Did AFK take him? Desha and RJ are talking among themselves, not concerned with our conversation.

"We tell our children they can be anything they want in life. We also tell our kids not to follow after anybody, but be a leader. But the second one of us becomes a leader, thinks for him or herself, or does something different. Boom! Excommunicated," Hakeem continues looking at the dirt mound.

"Sounds like a cult," Mya remarks and a brief smile appears on Hakeem's face.

"It is, but worse. You can change religions, you can change jobs, you can change political party affiliations, but you can't change race," Hakeem remarks.

"Sounds like coming out," Mya says in a low tone.

"What you mean? They're two different things," Hakeem says.

"Not too different," Mya answers. "My family is divided down the middle between Catholic and 7th Day Adventist. What my whole family believes is that being gay is a bad thing. When I came out to my family, I was excommunicated from them. No Christmas, no Thanksgiving, no Easter, no Sunday mass, no Saturday church services, no family reunion conversations, not even a decent conversation about dead relatives."

"That's horrible," I say as I feel a tremendous amount of guilt about her feelings.

"This was all because I felt a way about a person, and not the type of person they wanted me to. I have limited family in this country, and I'm cut off from them. My family that still lives in Nicaragua hates me," Mya mentions as more people leave from the gravesite.

"Hate is an extreme word," I say as Mya nods in agreement.

"My abuela spit in my face the last time I saw her and called me a disgrace. That's why it's hard when I see the disconnect between the LGBTQ community and the black community," Mya says in a low tone.

"I don't really think there's a disconnect between the two," Hakeem says.

"There is," Mya responds quickly.

"Growing up we had several gay neighbors. We had a lesbian couple that lived next door and a gay man across the street. One of the women from the lesbian couple was my bus driver growing up. She taught me pick up lines. We never thought nothing of their sexuality growing up. One of the guys, Mr. Mack, used to help my mom with the groceries and stuff all the time," Hakeem says defensively.

"That doesn't mean it's like that everywhere. That doesn't mean they don't live in fear of being attacked, judged or ridiculed. That doesn't mean they don't feel shame," Mya rebuts.

"Where did the LGBTQ community live for decades and feel safe? In the black communities. Where did they go to church? In the black communities. Where did they shop and eat? In the black communities. When did the disconnect start? I'm lost on that. I see what happens in the Arts District in contrast to what happens on School Side, The Ridgely Homes and the Market Place areas of Ridgely Square. The disconnect is with y'all against us. Y'all have the power, and we are fighting to have something," Hakeem yells, still in a defensive tone.

"I'm sorry it seems that way, but that's not what's happening at all. We see the NAACP and other organizations fighting for you all, and we are fighting to receive equal and fair treatment. I'm not trying to attack you, Dr. Andrews. I didn't mean to strike a chord, especially on this day that you're mourning your brother's death."

"No," Hakeem says as he pauses to think. "Being completely honest, I don't know everything about your struggle. As a Latinx woman, or as an openly lesbian woman. It just hurts when you say we have a disconnect with your community. When people like Tyrone Clinton or Kennard Lyles-Bey were murdered, we received no support and had to march. When people like Silk were murdered, the mayor got involved."

"The mayor only got involved because of you, fighting for us. They didn't care about Silk. Her own parents, the Littles, tried to cremate her without letting the public know. Black gay and black trans lives matter. There is a disconnect in our own community. But we need to get to a place where we can all put our resources together to move mountains," Mya returns.

"The Flamingo Club has done a lot of work in the Arts District, but not once have they attempted to help restore and save the rest of Ridgely Square," Hakeem says, his voice tense.

Silence falls upon the two as the rain begins to fall heavily. The mound of light brown dirt starts to turn to mud and runs into the grass.

"We should really meet and converse about this," Mya breaks the silence and says in a low tone. "We are on the same side of this war for equality, but we're fighting each other. I believe you know that."

Mya hugs Hakeem and me before walking to her car. Desha and RJ walk towards Hakeem's car as I look at the gravesite of my friend and would be brother-in-law.

I touch Mya's arm to stop her from walking away and ask her, "Did it ever get better with your family?"

"When I didn't talk about a person I was into, or something I was fighting for. My family talked. It's not like I was accepted in my church or truly loved the same again. I didn't want approval or anything special. Honestly, I didn't need them or the church to accept me. I just wanted love from my family. I just wanted the option to worship at my church without feeling like an outcast in the middle of a crowded room. So I was isolated. Even among other members of my community now, I'm isolated. I'm from Nicaragua. I'm a first generation American citizen. I get called names like illegal, even though I've lived the majority of my life in this country. I really want to tell you it gets better, but it doesn't," Mya answers, walking away to her car as Detective Murphy and Agent Parker approach Hakeem and me.

"Dr. Andrews, I'm sorry for your loss," Agent Parker says as Detective Murphy looks me over.

"Ms. Gibbons, would you mind coming with us? You're not under arrest, we just want to ask you some questions," Detective Murphy says in a forceful tone.

"About what?" Hakeem questions in an angry tone.

"Dr. Andrews, this is in relation to the ongoing investigation of the Alphas and possibly AFK," Detective Murphy answers. I agree.

"Again, you're not under arrest," Detective Murphy says as they walk me towards a black sports utility vehicle. "For formality and safety purposes I have to handcuff you from the back, Ms. Gibbons. It's not that you're under arrest. It's just for our safety to ride to our investigative building."

"I can get a ride there. You don't have to handcuff me," I respond in fear of what is happening.

"Ms. Gibbons, you're not under arrest," Detective Murphy assures me as I take a step back. Agent Parker stands quietly, never making a statement or looking in my direction.

"My fiancé, Hakeem Andrews, will take me to the station. You're not going to handcuff me if I'm innocent, and you're not going to handcuff me in front of my children. Somebody burned my house down! Did you catch them? My daughter, Trinity Gibbons, she's in the burn victims unit right now. Did you get the person who did that to her? Are you bringing them to justice? Hakeem's brother is not even cold in the ground yet, did

you get his murderer? You're here trying to handcuff me,"
I scream as loud as I can.

"Ms. Gibbons, we're not trying to cause a scene. We
just want to transport you. You can get in the back without
the cuffs, would that be OK?" Detective Murphy asks.

"Let her ride up front with me, you ride in the back,"
Agent Parker says as Detective Murphy appears angered
by the statement. Agent Parker opens the door for me as
Detective Murphy searches me for weapons.

"Ma'am this is just a formality," Detective Murphy says
with a dismissive tone. "It's only fair, you did kill your
father a couple years ago."

"That was uncalled for," Bell's disembodied voice
whispers in my ear.

"Where is the former police commissioner, Alex
Tillman?" I ask as Detective Murphy quickly answers that
he is spending time with his family.

Chapter 17

Time appears to fly and then stand still as I sit in the interrogation room. The investigation unit is in an office building where several other detectives work. I notice homicides and special victims units along with several interrogation rooms. There are tons of cubicles with clutter, files, awards, action figures and figurines throughout the building. The carpet beneath the desks and cubicles appears to be new.

There is a medium size metal table in the center of the interrogation room with a large steel ring attached to the top. The room has cameras placed at the top corners of the office. The temperature in the room is unusually cold but doesn't have a smell to it. The tile on the floor is extremely clean and a bright white color. Detective Murphy and Agent Parker sit across from me with several files piled up on a chair on Murphy's side.

"You know, I was recently promoted to detective, Ms. Gibbons," Detective Murphy says. The lighting in the room does not do him any favors. I can see the wrinkles in his face and the yellow in his eyes and teeth that I never noticed before.

"I should thank you for that," Detective Murphy continues, "When Bell and some of the other NAFA goons were brought up on charges, I was promoted. I was an officer for 24 years before I finally received a promotion. I guess I owe you and your aunt a huge thank you."

"Is that why you brought me here? To tell me about your recent accomplishment?" I ask as Murphy gives a half smile and nods side-to-side. I feel a cold chill in the air and wish I could have gone home to change out of my dress and into some jeans or a sweatsuit.

"No. Sadly, I was assigned to the Homicide Investigative Team, and the reason why you're here is because we're just trying to make some things make sense," Murphy says as Agent Parker appears annoyed with his partner.

"About my father?" I ask, fearful. I can feel my heart pumping out my chest. I know they will eventually lock me up. It's been in the back of my mind since after the State's Attorney, Jada Austin said she was going to drop the charges, and then was murdered by AFK.

"That's not on the top of the charts. Can you tell us what you know about the Action Figure Killer?" Murphy asks in a serious tone. I force out a loud exhale and my fear leaves before concern and racing thoughts re-enter my mind.

"Nothing much. He murdered a lot of people in the community, like gang members. He also murdered the state's attorney and the former city councilman," I answer, wondering why I'm being questioned.

"He also murdered the former mayor and our police chief," Murphy says.

I sit quietly, wondering where the line of questions will go next. My thoughts race to Jamar, and witness him lying on the ground and then watch Bell being murdered in front of my face. I think about my father for a brief moment until I hear Bell's voice telling me to stop.

"You know that there is a copycat killer, right?" Murphy asks and I nod in agreement. "How many people did you tell about the copycat AFK?"

"Nobody!" I answer. I thought something must have gotten out. Are they going to pin this on me? I can't afford to go to prison, not now. Trinity is in the burn unit, I have two businesses to run and four children to raise. My mind continues to run as Bell's voice keeps telling me to calm down. I hear my grandmother's voice telling me to take deep breaths.

"Do you know who AFK is?" Murphy asks in an annoyed tone.

"No!" I answer as Parker turns his face towards Murphy.

"You know something!" Murphy screams.

"Detective, we're just trying to rule her out," Agent Parker says as Murphy dismisses him.

"She's manipulating us. She got away with killing her father, and she's not going to stop," Murphy says as he slams two folders in front of me.

"I'm not AFK, or the fake AFK," I respond as I think about something my mother said before. She previously mentioned that when I was younger I blacked out and said I was someone else. Could this be one of those scenarios where I was AFK the whole time? Oh my God. I'm AFK.

"No, you're not," Bell answers. "Be smarter than that. You didn't kill all those people. Your dad, yes, but not all those people. Where did you get the green Army man toys from? You don't have any. The kids don't even play with those."

Remember when I used to stand in the basement and lose track of time? What if I am committing murders?

"Stop it! That's not your story," Bell says in my ear as Murphy takes pictures out of the folders and places them on the table.

"You opened your restaurant, Legacy of Florence, gained a home and got a nice inheritance from your grandmother. You also started a bank with your fiancé. Under the shadow of legit business, I think you have been washing money for the Alphas, or getting paid to commit murders for the Alphas and then washing the money to make it look like a legal operation," Murphy says as Parker shakes his head in disagreement.

"Why the hell would I do that?" I ask, feeling insulted. "Paul Douglass has made several attempts to use my companies as a front for his drug and sex trafficking operations. I have told him no each time. The last time he did it, it cost Jamar his life."

"Funny you should mention that," Murphy says as he slides a picture over to me on the table of my father's corpse in my basement from the shooting. He also slides a picture of the handgun I used and pictures of fingerprints with circles around certain points of the prints.

"The gun you used to kill your father. The same one you said you grabbed from your father and used in self-defense, had his prints, your prints and Jamar's prints.

How and why did that gun have Jamar's prints?" Murphy asks, pointing at the pictures of the prints.

"I don't know. I can't answer that," I respond as Agent Parker's posture changes, and he looks at me suspiciously.

"You're lying," Bell says, laughing and cackling in my head. "Jamar gave you that gun. You didn't wrestle it from your father. You also didn't have to kill him. You made that choice. It felt good didn't it? *Didn't It!* You freed yourself from the shadow of your father the second you pulled that trigger. You said it was to protect your children, but it was to avenge what your father took from you."

"It was!" I scream out loud as Parker and Murphy look on, confused as to who I was speaking with.

"You don't need an insanity defense. You're not under arrest," Murphy says as he places another folder on the desk.

"Are you ok, Ms. Gibbons?" Parker asks, and I nod yes. I feel so embarrassed. I feel like the walls are closing in around me. I'm going to get locked up. Why did I listen to Bell? He's not even real.

"Jamar was one of the founding members of the 10th Bank. Did you cut him out to get a bigger cut? You founded the bank with his brother Hakeem, Allen Bradley and Clair from Nubian Media," Murphy says as he glances briefly at Agent Parker in disgust.

"Why would I want to kill Jamar? My kids loved him, he was like a real brother to me. He loved his brother Hakeem. He did so much for the people in Ridgely Square," I state as Murphy slides a picture of Jamar's body towards me. It was from the day he was murdered. The image on the page is the image that is etched in my mind. The memory I've had since Darrin showed me Jamar's body.

"You were the first one to find him, am I right, Ms. Gibbons?" Murphy asks. I nod my head yes.

"Can you say that out loud, Ms. Gibbons?" Murphy asks as his voice lowers.

"Yes, Hakeem and I were the first to see him," I answer as Murphy takes more pictures out his folders. "You're not under arrest, Ms. Gibbons, we're just talking. We're all friends here. We're just trying to solve this case and finish this investigation with the Alphas. You want to help us, right? You're my friend, right Tiffany? Is it ok for me to call you Tiffany?"

I nod yes as Agent Parker rolls his eyes at Murphy.

"Councilman Dawson was murdered too," Murphy continues as he slides pictures of his body towards me. The public never saw pictures of his body. The scene is grotesque, with the posturing. There is a plastic bag over his head in addition to all of the blood.

"AFK has another pattern aside from the toys, Tiffany. Do you know what that is?" Murphy asks.

"I don't know, the grocery bag over his head?" I guess in a confused and nervous tone. The air in the room is thick. I can taste metal in my mouth. I want to cry, but I did nothing wrong. Do I look innocent? I am innocent of these murders, but do I look guilty?

"You're doing great," Bell says in my ear.

"That's right. The public doesn't know about the plastic bags, and we purposely withheld that from you. Why did you put the three bags over his head? Why did you specifically put three bags over almost all of your victims' heads. What does three represent? Is it some kind of ADHD tic for you? Does it get you off sexually?" Murphy fires off the questions in rapid succession.

"It wasn't me," I say.

"What does three represent?" Murphy asks again. "Your grandmother and your fiancé are religious, does the number three have significance in the Bible?"

"It means perfection and completion in the Bible," I answer, looking down at the table.

"Hey, you're not in trouble, Tiffany. We're just talking. Nobody is locking you up. Just help us out and you can go. You want to go home, right?" Murphy asks as he places another folder on the desk.

"The police chief, Junior Dawson, why did you kill him? Was it because you felt he didn't protect you enough from the Alphas and Marshawn Bell?" Murphy continues as he shows me crime scene photos from his murder.

"Anna Cartwright, she publicly humiliated your friend Sasha Greene years ago following her son's botched robbery of a carryout. Was that a vengeance kill? Or was that a door prize because you couldn't murder Clair? The 10th Bank is doing great and one less person at the top is good for your wallet," Murphy states as I think about Darrin. He's AFK! Not me, it's him. I better take this charge. At least he'll have a fighting chance at life.

"Hey Tiffany, help us out. This FBI agent is costing taxpayers a lot of money. You're tired of the Alpha investigation, just like us. You just wanted to help out. Rid the streets of Baltimore of bad people. These people sold drugs, killed people, kidnapped and sold girls. They doped up, pimped out young girls and made them have sex with people against their will," Murphy says as he shows pictures of a large number of deceased gang members with bags over their heads and green Army men toys lying at their sides.

"You were trying to help us out. Let us help you out. You're a hero, you're one of us. We wouldn't even have known about the bad people from NAFA or Marshawn Bell if it wasn't for you. Let us help you. Tell us what we can do to help you," Murphy asks as there is a knock on the door and a tall, moderately chubby African American man with a gray suit enters the room. He has salt and pepper colored hair, with a thick mustache. He appears to be in his early-to-mid 50s.

"Don't say another word, Ms. Gibbons," the man says with a very deep and booming voice.

"Oh this guy. Not a good look for you, Ms. Gibbons," Murphy says as he looks at the man in the suit. Parker appears puzzled by the whole scene.

"Oh this guy, indeed," the man responds back to Detective Murphy.

"I'm sorry, who is this?" I ask, feeling that this is some ruse of good cop, bad cop.

"I'm your lawyer, Ms. Gibbons," the man says as I feel more confused. I didn't ask for a lawyer and I never met this man a day in my life.

"This fine gentleman is Vernon Shaw, a lawyer that works with scum, like the Alphas. He's your representative," Murphy says as his tone and posture change to a more upright and annoyed presentation.

"He's not my lawyer," I scream as Vernon Shaw walks closer to me.

"I would like everything she previously said stripped from the record," Vernon demands.

"Not a problem, she's not under arrest," Murphy says, and he leans back in his chair and folds his arms.

"Did they read you your Miranda rights?" Vernon asks. I look at him confused. "Your right to remain silent, anything you say can and will be used against you in a court of law. You have the right to an attorney…. that stuff?"

"No," I answer.

"She's not under arrest," Murphy yells at Vernon.

"So she's free to go, am I correct?" Vernon asks as Parker walks to the door and opens it for Vernon and me, signaling we can leave.

"Ms. Gibbons, this isn't a good look for you. We're trying to help you," Murphy says as Vernon pushes me out the door.

Murphy continues to yell out the door at me, as Vernon escorts me out. "Your house was just burned down. You were kidnapped by Marshawn Bell. Your aunt, Gina Simms is in witness protection. Your best friend, Sasha Greene, stays in rehab and chooses to not come home. A high-ranking Alpha member was shot and killed right in front of your house 2 years ago. You killed your father on a breaking and entering charge with a loaded handgun that you magically wrestled away. Why are you at the center of all this drama? What are you not telling us? I'm trying to help you, Tiffany!"

"You couldn't back me up just one time?" Murphy then screams at Parker.

"She wasn't AFK. Also, the purpose of my investigation is to get as much information about the Alphas as I can and bring them to justice. Until we can get the head of the gang, we're just wasting time here," Parker answers.

"What about AFK?" Murphy questions.

"I figure that AFK will lead Paul Douglass to us. He will take a deal, or slip up. I'm sure your years on the force will lead to the capture of AFK. You don't need the FBI for this guy, who basically crippled the whole Alpha operation himself," Parker says, walking out of the room and watching me and Vernon walk down the hallway towards the elevator.

"You think you know everything," Murphy replies. "Let me borrow that big brain of yours so you can tell me if this bump is an ingrown hair, cancer, or herpes."

Chapter 18

Less than half an hour later I arrive in Vernon Shaw's law office. The glass on the front door has Shaw Legal inscribed in gold Times New Roman lettering. Immediately as I walk inside of the building, I am standing in the waiting room that has several bookshelves with law books against the right wall. In the middle of the waiting room is leather furniture, a long table, and the rear waiting room area is sealed off by a glass door and wall.

To the left of the front door is a staircase, and next to that is a door that opens to a bathroom. Sitting on one of the brown leather sofas next to the closed glass office door is Paul. Standing in front of the closed off office door is Roland with a double-barrel shotgun in hand. The shotgun has a black pistol grip clasped tightly in Roland's right hand as the barrel rests on his left palm. The office smells like incense, coffee and leather threw a party and no decent self-respecting woman's olfactory nerves are invited.

"It took a lot to get you here," Paul says as he leans back into the sofa. There is an open magazine with a local rapper on the cover.

"Sorry, I had an unscheduled visit with Baltimore City's finest," I joke back as Paul gives a smile in response.

"Not only do you have a nice ass, but you have a good sense of humor. Another good quality," Paul says with a childish grin. My smile dissolves into visible disgust for his comment.

"C'mon, Tiffy. If I entered you into the Preakness, nobody would be able to tell your ass from the actual horses competing. You could have made some great money working with me," Paul continues as if he's just given me a badge of honor.

"I look at how you wore those jeans at your restaurant, how the dress you have on fits you and your walk, Tiffy. That gap in your walk and how you stand. I'm willing to wager you have a Hemi under that hood," Paul says then he laughs loudly.

"A what?" I question. I have heard a lot of lewd remarks in my life, a large majority coming from my father and my twins' father, but I have never heard that one.

"A Chrysler Hemi is an engine. It is one of the best engines in the world. What I'm saying is, I think there's something special about you sexually, and if you would lose about 20 to 25 pounds, maybe do some sit-ups, a lot of men would pay top dollar for it," Paul continues to say as if I should appreciate his words. I'm 5'4 and weigh 145 pounds and never thought of myself as overweight.

"I don't drive, so I don't get the engine reference, but I'm very happy with how I look and the person that I'm with," I answer as Paul motions to Vernon Shaw.

"Mr. Shaw, can you pick us up some food? Roland and I will take the regular from that steakhouse you and your wife like going to. And can you pick Tiffy up a garden salad with a light vinaigrette? We don't want Pillsbury to get high blood pressure," Paul orders while laughing to himself. He laughs by himself as nobody else's facial expression changes. I'm very insulted that he keeps talking about my weight. I wish I had that gun I shot my father with so I could put a bullet through him as he sits on the chair.

"You could slap him. Well, that wouldn't be a good idea because Roland Wise, a.k.a. The Chocolate Punisher, might kill you," Bell says into my ear as I chuckle out loud. The laughter appears to upset Paul. He turns back towards me with a sharp soul piercing look.

Vernon leaves the office building and locks the door behind him without saying a word to Paul or Roland. Paul slowly crosses his left leg, resting the ankle over his right knee as he begins reading the magazine that is sitting at his side. It is in that moment I notice Paul doesn't have shoes on. He has on colorfully-designed socks.

Silence fills the room for a brief moment as I stand near the front bookshelf and Roland watches me with the shotgun in hand. The only sound in the room is the torrential rain pouring violently onto the roof and the random chirp from a smoke detector. Paul breaks the silence as he sets the magazine down for a brief moment.

"This has to be awkward for you, Tiffy. The last time you saw Roland he turned your home into a s'more. Who do you wish you had shot and killed more, your father or this guy?" Paul says, pointing at Roland before looking back at the magazine. His facial expression is relaxed as if there is nothing to worry about.

"Can I sit down?" I ask. Paul motions for me to sit in one of the leather chairs near the bathroom. I cross my legs in an attempt to get comfortable in the chair. Paul already objectifies women, the last thing I need to do is to give him a free show.

"Why am I here?" I ask, as my mind races. Why am I alive? Why did the lawyer just leave us in his office building?

"You had value to me, Tiffy. Sadly, that value has decreased," Paul says, setting the magazine down next to him on the couch. "The bank, and the restaurant, both great places to wash money. You and Hakeem were so far off the radar of the FBI, it was perfect. Nobody would have questioned anything."

"It would have tarnished our reputation," I explain to Paul as I glance at Roland, still holding the shotgun with a firm grip.

"No, nobody would have known," Paul counters.

"Why don't you just turn yourself in? The FBI would be glad to give you a deal," I suggest as Paul smirks.

"I'm not a snitch. They would want information, and too many important people would go down if I go down," Paul counters, while picking the magazine back up.

"So you wanted to wash your money through my bank and restaurant knowing the FBI is watching you. Why take down my legit company in the midst of your problems?" I ask as Paul glances at Roland.

"Do you like history, Tiffy?" Paul asks as he flips through the pages of the magazine. "It's a huge mixture of the truth and facts that the winners of wars want told."

"What does that have to do with anything?" I ask as Roland walks towards the door to look outside.

"Bishop Kiesha Stokes, the good Reverend Dr. Hakeem Andrews's adopted sister. Do you know who she is?" Paul asks as I nod my head.

"An amazing accountant, stock trader, and she runs mega churches throughout the United States and several countries in Africa, South America, and Asia," Paul continues. "She gave your bank seed money, and referred a lot of customers to you. A lot of that money in your institution is my money. Properly invested in your bank."

"What are you talking about?" I ask, at a total loss for words.

"You wanted to take the high road, and turned us down. We were testing you, especially since you took money from us in the past," Paul boasts.

"What money did I knowingly take from y'all in the past?" I ask as I feel the hairs on my neck stand up. I feel goose bumps on my arms. I feel trapped. All I can think about are my kids, what example I once thought I was setting for them, and how this person just made that into a lie.

"The Detective Sergeant Marshawn Bell gave you millions of dollars the night of his death. That money was from me. I'm willing to bet that you used some of that money to open your little bank and your restaurant. You did it without raising an eyebrow because of your grandmother's inheritance. History is interesting when you know how to read it, isn't it, Tiffy?" Paul asks as he goes back to reading the magazine again.

"Where did you get that idea from?" I ask, concerned and fearful.

"Sasha Greene, your former roommate and best friend since middle school. We got to her and made her a couple of promises for her safety. She provided us some good insight into your aunt Gina, Marshawn Bell and your piss-poor parenting skills. I helped create the scenario that if she would find your aunt and get me the information, then she would be allowed to live. Of course she wasn't easy to break, she really loves you like a sister. But when I threatened to kill you and your children before finally taking her life, she told us everything," Paul says, then he is silent again.

"Remember what Jamar use to say?" I heard my cousin Tina whisper in my ear.

"You can't live in the Promised Land until you slaughter the people that are already living in the Promised Land," Bell answers.

"He's the person that's blocking us from the Promised Land." Tina proclaims.

"Whatever it takes, we take him out," Bell says.

"Amen," my grandmother interjects.

"Why did you put your dirty money in my bank?" I ask. Paul slams the magazine on the couch next to him.

"You're not going to let me read in peace!" Paul yells as Roland walks over to me.

"Get ready!" Bell shouts in my ear.

"I need to know, why me?" I ask with my heart pounding out my chest. My eyes watch Roland's hands as they grip the shotgun.

"Your plan is to piss him off?" Tina questions.

"No. We're going to lure Paul into a false sense of security. He thinks Tiffany is weak," Bell answers.

"You were safe," Paul says in a lower tone. "You were in good standing with the police department after the takedown of NAFA, and some of my people. Good for you. Also, Kiesha Stokes needed somewhere to spread her money around. Somewhere people would celebrate her for it. You'd be surprised where she gets her money from. A kingpin locked up makes a huge donation to the church, nobody bats an eye. A cartel boss makes a donation to her mission, nobody bats an eye. Her work also makes it easy to move tons of heroin, fentanyl, girls and cocaine from country to country."

"Why my bank?" I ask as Paul stands up and walks towards me.

"Because of Hakeem and Jamar. She hated Jamar because he was the family embarrassment. She hated Hakeem because no matter what she did, Hakeem got the public's attention. She took over their father's church, Hakeem advocated for black unarmed youth gunned down by the police. She got married, Hakeem went to school to get a doctorate degree. Family issues can be tiring. For me, plain and simple, you stole from me. Money, power and fear is what I live by," Paul says as he slaps me and places his hands around my neck, choking me.

"You have the nerve to think you're better than me. You took my money! You thought the FBI and the police were going to take my power! Marshawn Bell tried to take this power from me! I have to remind my people who the hell I am!" Paul says in a forceful tone, choking me and pressing his weight into me before releasing his grip. I gasp for air as he slaps me along the left side of my face.

"Your father, Cube, was supposed to get the kids from your house. I was going to hold them as ransom to get back the money that you had. Of course, you killed him and that plan went downhill. So I had to think of something else. I was just going to kill you, but when word got out that Jamar and Hakeem were starting a bank to invest in the community, a new opportunity presented itself."

I attempt to punch Paul, but he blocks my punch and greets my chin with a more powerful swing of the fist. The force of the punch hurts my teeth and my ears, knocking me to the couch. Paul then places his knee on my neck as he takes the shotgun from Roland and places the barrel against my forehead.

"History, it is not always true. You made people believe that your restaurant was a good investment with an inheritance. There are so many black-owned businesses with loans from banks from a strong, independent honest black woman and her God-fearing fiancé. In truth, you're a money launderer, and if I go down, so do all those businesses. So do you. Which makes you and the true Legacy of Florence a fraud," Paul says with an unhinged tone.

"Now tell me, what side of the aisle do you stand on? The side where the history is a powerful and uplifting story that has blessed countless people, or the side where the truth comes out and so many people suffer?" Paul asks, looking at the pain on my face. My face is on fire. It's hard for me to breathe. I can't really focus on the words that he is saying because I keep thinking about the failure I've become. Just for trying to do the right thing.

"Paul, look at this," Roland says, showing Paul his phone. Paul removes the pressure of his knee from my neck and hands Roland the shotgun. Roland points the gun at me. Paul goes back to the couch and sits down, stunned, next to the magazine.

"Here's the other thing about history, Tiffy," Paul begins as the tone of his voice completely shifts to something else. Concern. "The Action Figure Killer. That wasn't my creation. I was clearing the chessboard of loose ends. People that were talking to the FBI and the police. The prostitutes that would snitch, the low level drug pushers, the rappers, anybody that was affiliated with me that would point in my direction. I murdered. Then this guy, AFK, came along. He killed everybody. Making it a living hell for my network. And now, he just killed my lawyer."

"What lawyer?" I ask, only knowing about the person whose office we are in.

"Vernon Shaw! I thought you was just fat, I didn't know you was dumb too," Paul says, rolling his eyes.

"We need to leave here," Roland says and Paul agrees.

"Are you going to just lay there after that ass whipping?" Bell's voice says in anger. Not even a second later I hear my grandmother's voice in agreement with him.

"He's not better than you," my grandmother's voice says. "Get up and whip his ass. Even if he is stronger, he will respect you! You're my grandchild. You survived your father. You are raising four kids! Is this what you're raising them to be? Cowards? No. Fight back."

As I cough and gasp for air I look for an item to hit Paul with and locate a heavy glass award. I throw it at his head, connecting as it makes a loud thump. I chase and tackle him to the floor. I swing wildly at his head, as I connect left hand after right hand. He attempts to fight back as I scratch him, claw at his eyes and scream in rage.

"You tried to take down my company! You tried to destroy my family's name! You called me fat!" I yell.

"You really needed that salad," Paul says as Roland pulls me off. I try to pull away from Roland and notice the shotgun on the couch. Before I can get to it, the lights to the office turn off.

"That's not from the rain! He's here," Bell says, alluding to AFK.

"Get out of here, now!" Roland says, grabbing his shotgun as a loud bang is heard breaking the glass barrier between the waiting room and the office. I hide behind one of the couches as Paul hides in the bathroom. Roland crouches down by the table, pointing the shotgun towards the office.

A rolling sound is heard on the ground, over the shattered glass moments before a loud bang and a flash. I am temporarily blinded and my balance is unsteady. I hear the sounds of a scuffle and I'm unsure of what happened as I try to regain my vision. I remember smelling smoke and hearing a few shots fired. As my vision comes back, a large white cloud fills the law office and glass is all over the floor. A stocky male is present and fighting Roland.

I glance towards Paul, who is also having a hard time gaining his composure after the bright flash. I hear the voices of my grandmother and Bell yelling at me as I glance at Paul's silhouette. Thoughts of my mother, and how she ignored my cries for help as a child overcome me. I grab the lamp from the table and charge towards Paul in the bathroom, hitting him as hard as I can. As he falls flat on the bathroom floor, I continue to hit him multiple times.

I think of all the times my mother called me a liar when I told her about my father's sexual assaults as I place his head in the toilet bowl, attempting to drown him as he struggles to fight back.

"He's mine!" I hear someone say as he chokes Roland in a sleeper hold. The person is dressed in all black, in what appears to be riot gear style clothes. Roland struggles as I hit Paul again with the lamp, leaving him on the bathroom floor. Several police sirens wail, heading our way as the person stands over Roland's body, dropping several green toy Army men over his back. He places three grocery bags over Roland's head before firing the shotgun several times into his chest area.

"Leave now, Ms. Gibbons," the voice says as I look down at Paul struggling to get to his feet. I have a large shard of glass in my hand, ready to stab him in the back as thoughts of my home and Trinity run through my mind. I feel anger burn like fire in my eyes, hands and through my veins.

"Leave now," the man demands as he walks near the large, stained table and the furniture. The office is extremely smokey and the only light is coming from outside. I run out of the law office. Instantly, several swat officers run into the building. An officer places handcuffs on me and makes me get on my knees, on the sidewalk, before Detective Murphy and Agent Parker walk toward me.

"Take her out the cuffs," Murphy says to the officer as Paul is brought out of the building in handcuffs. I am shocked that Paul is still alive and was not killed by the man.

"You ready to start working with us?" Agent Parker asks as Paul grins at me.

"What happened to your face?" Detective Murphy asks Paul, who is bleeding profusely from his face and neck. His suit clothes are soaked with blood and water.

"You should see what I did to the other guy," Paul says as the officer uncuffs him.

"Who did this to you?" Murphy asks as Paul begins walking away.

"Your guess is about as good as mine. Am I under arrest for visiting my lawyer?" Paul asks as several officers look at him.

"You should probably hang around for medical attention," an officer says as Paul waves his hand at the officer in a dismissive manner.

"Your lawyer was murdered a few minutes ago, right around the corner from here," Murphy says to Paul as he walks off. "Did you have anything to do with that?"

"It was done by AFK," another detective says to Paul, as he shrugs his shoulders. "He murdered your friend in there too. Did he assault you two?"

"Talk to her. I don't talk to 12," Paul says as he continues to walk away.

"What the hell is 12?" Murphy asks as a police officer told him that it was another name for police. "But 9 plus 1 plus 1 equals 11; where the hell does 12 come from?"

"Did AFK do that to you, Ms. Gibbons?" Agent Parker asks, pointing towards the bruises on my face and my neck.

"Did you guys get him? He was in there. I think he murdered Roland," I say as my adrenaline begins to lower. I begin feeling tired, and start noticing aches and pains from the assault Paul gave me. I also notice broken glass in my palms and arms. My hands also start to swell, and my eye feels like it's on fire. I have blood dripping from my palms and my mouth and several officers look in my direction in awe that I survived the AFK attack.

"We didn't, but we can confirm that he did kill Roland Wise," Agent Parker says with a look of concern on his face. The rain continues to fall and I begin to notice tears and rips in my black dress.

"You didn't see anything? You can't tell us how he looks or anything?" Murphy asks with a look of confusion.

"He used some kind of flash grenade and smoke bomb before he began his assault. He had a very authoritative voice. He was strong, very strong. That's all I can tell you," I say as Parker guides me to an SUV with an open door.

"I just want to get back to the hospital to see my daughter. Can someone call Hakeem, and make sure that my kids are with him?" I ask as Murphy nods in agreement.

Chapter 19

Inside of the SUV, Detective Murphy drives as Agent Parker rides in the back seat. I sit in the front passenger seat looking out the window as the rain continues to fall. As we sit at a red light, Detective Murphy and I watch as two young males talk on the corner before they get into an old model Crown Victoria with temporary paper license plate tags. The car then drives off quickly.

"We got off on the wrong foot," Detective Murphy says, breaking the silence in the car.

"This case has been tiring. We have the FBI working this Alpha case, and then we have AFK blowing everything to kingdom come. I just can't catch a break," Murphy says as I sit in silence. I don't have a thought. I would like to tell you I was thinking about my kids, or my home, or my restaurant, or the bank, or my mother. My mind was actually blank. Like I released something in me when I was fighting Paul. It almost felt euphoric, knowing I'd fought back and won.

"Can you tell me what the hell happened in there?" Murphy asks as the light turns green. "I honestly don't believe you're associated with the Alphas in any way. I'm going to lay my cards on the table here. The thing is, why did they send a lawyer for you? Then, why did that lawyer wind up dead? Why did Paul Douglass's personal henchman, Roland freaking Wise get murdered by AFK? Then somehow, by the grace of God, you and Paul survive. How did you make it out of there? And no offence, you're a very beautiful lady, but you look like you went through a war zone. What happened in there?"

The silence in my head continues. I don't hear the voices of my grandmother, or Bell, or my deceased daughter Kenya. I don't hear my deceased cousin Tina. Nothing. Not a thought, not a care. I am at peace with everything. I don't care about anything around me.

"Ms. Gibbons?" Agent Parker says my name repeatedly in a concerned tone. I snap out of whatever trance I was in, and notice the street lights and the rain falling. I am able to see the shapes of each drop as they appear to fall in slow motion. I snap out of the trance once more as I hear Agent Parker call my name again.

"Sorry," I finally respond. Searching for the words to say to explain my behavior, I can't think of anything to follow up with.

"You've had a long day, I get it," Murphy says as he stops at another red light. "Your daughter's in the burn unit, your mother is in hospice, your house was set on fire and you just went to a funeral a couple hours ago. What is going on with Paul? Why did he send his scumbag lawyer to get you from the station? May God rest his soul."

"He wants to wash his dirty money with our bank and with my restaurant," I answer. I begin thinking about my son, Darrin. He was angry about my encounters and communication with the police. Maybe I am talking to them too much. Maybe this should stop. Maybe I'm making things worse.

"Do you have any details about what he's doing with the money now, Ms. Gibbons?" Agent Parker asks, leaning forward in his seat to talk closer to me. I feel uncomfortable about this. Rightfully so, I'm in a car with two strangers, and now they're acting like they really are interested in what I know. My dad used to do this to me before he would rape me when my mother was at work.

"I really don't have any information to pass on," I answer as my mind begins to wonder about Paul, and what makes him tick. "What do y'all know about Paul?" I ask.

Agent Parker leans back in the chair and answers first. "He's the head of the Alphas. I'm told he was orphaned at

3 months old and his father was murdered at some point while his mother was pregnant. She died from an overdose. He grew up in the foster care system. It is believed that he was on the spectrum for Asperger's, but never had an official diagnosis. He has a strange fixation or phobia about women over his ideal weight. That weight often varies by height."

Murphy then places chewing tobacco in his mouth as he sits at a red light, moments before Parker continues giving me Paul's disposition. "He ran away several times from multiple foster families, and dropped out of school when he was 15 years old. He was in and out of children's detention centers. He disappeared off the radar for a while and popped back up with bachelor's and master's degrees in business and administration. He graduated summa cum laude from George Washington University. Since that time he has run the Alphas like a fine-tuned machine."

"I have tried for years to put this guy away, as a police officer and a detective," Murphy interjects.

"If Marshawn Bell and the good folks of the Narcotics and Firearms Task Force weren't so crooked, you probably would have nailed him," I comment as Murphy makes an audible exhale through his nose.

"Why do you hate cops so much?" Murphy asks me, catching me off guard.

"Who said I hate cops?" I respond sharply.

"You and your aunt were on TV dragging us down. You got your wish and brought down NAFA. Before then, your fiancé was on TV trashing us for doing our jobs," Murphy answers.

"Let's unpack everything you said. My aunt dragged me into the whole NAFA thing. I wanted nothing to do with it. I just wanted to raise my kids, finish college and work as a social worker. I have no problems with police, my grandfather was a police officer that died in the line of duty. My friend from church, and Tyrone Clinton's football coach, Edward Carter was a police officer. He was murdered by the Alphas. Interestingly enough, the detective, Marshawn Bell, paid the Alphas to murder him. I don't hate cops. I just don't really trust them," I answer.

"What have we done for you to not trust us, aside from the whole NAFA thing?" Murphy continues to question.

"Aside from being profiled frequently? The night of my prom my date and I were pulled over, searched, had the rental car's carpet and chairs cut and ripped apart by police looking for drugs. They never found them and we were left with a bill. My senior class trip we had a swat unit called on us for going into a bank to make a cash withdrawal," I answer as Murphy rolls his eyes.

"None of those things happened," Murphy says, disgusted by my statements.

"Just as true as my father being a rapist and kidnapping kids for the Alphas," I respond as silence overtakes the car again.

A few minutes go by before Murphy asks another question. "How well did you know Edward Carter?"

"He was a great guy. He helped cut grass, and cleaned the church before my youngest daughter's father took on that responsibility," I answer. "He used to date this med student named Ciara."

"He was going to propose to her the day he was murdered by the Alphas," Murphy says in a solemn tone. "I knew Carter. I used to give him a hard time. He was always so damn positive, and optimistic. He was opinionated, but he was a good guy."

"Yeah, he was a really good guy," I agree in a low tone.

"I've wanted to get this off my chest for a while," Murphy says as he glances out the driver side window at a homeless person sitting on the curb drinking a soda. "I really hazed him bad during the end of his life. I don't know. He was really bright, and everybody liked him. I was the grizzled vet that time passed by. I was the idiot with a G.E.D. and tons of writeups. Carter was the future. When he died, it hit me. I was jealous of him, and I never would get a chance to apologize to him."

"I'm sure he would have forgiven you," I say, turning towards Murphy as he tries to resist becoming emotional.

"I don't deserve it. He didn't deserve to be murdered. It should have been me. I wish I was with him that day instead of the chief. I could have saved him, and we could have discussed our differences. We were still cops. We were still brothers. Brothers fight all the time. I know he would have had my back," Murphy says as we approach the hospital's entrance.

"You ever try to talk to someone about those feelings? I used to run a grief and loss support group at the Bradley Funeral Home," I say as Murphy parks.

"That therapy counseling stuff ain't for me. I got a bottle of whisky waiting on me when I get home. That and my westerns on the TV," Murphy answers as Parker points at a teenager shooting at a young adult man in front of the hospital.

"What the hell did we miss?" Murphy asks as he pulls away from the hospital entrance.

Parker glances at his phone for a moment before answering Murphy, "A few minutes ago Paul Douglass put out a message on several social media platforms to "paint Ridgely Square red." He started talking about the FBI investigation and members of the Alphas being snitches. He encouraged all loyal Alphas to kill every snitch and every non-Alpha member in his name."

"What is he… some kind of cult leader?" Murphy asks as a crowd of teenage boys gather in the front of the hospital.

"No, but he thinks he's a martyr. He said that he's willing to die in a blaze of glory rather than to snitch or give up any information related to the Alphas, or his accountant," Parker says, placing the phone back in his pocket.

"His accountant?" I say with the goal of exploring what they knew.

"That's classified information, Ms. Simms," Parker answers.

Several other young boys run into the hospital shooting at other young adult men, who soon return fire. I notice a young person's face running past the SUV before he is shot down. His name was Moose, I met him a couple weeks ago at the basketball court.

As Murphy drives to a safe location, several police sirens can be heard in concert with a large amount of gunfire. Some of the gunshots sound like assault rifles. As we drive around the block we witness several people being assaulted by poles, bats and bricks. I look out the passenger side window and see a group of young women fighting a man on cement steps by the front door.

"What the hell happened to this city?" I ask as a bullet hits the rear door of the SUV. A moment later two shots hit the rear window of the SUV.

"It's bullet proof," Murphy says as he drives faster and a person stands behind the car with a small handgun pointed at us. As the young male attempts to shoot, a person walks behind the young man and shoots him down with a shotgun.

"This is a mixture of Marshawn Bell and Paul Douglass. They messed up the balance of power with the gangs," Murphy says as he drives faster down another row of houses. It appears that more people are fighting outside of this community. Several homes are on fire, and a car was driven into the side of someone's home.

"The pills that the Alphas flooded the market with, along with the Cabal constantly being assaulted and killed without penalty, it caused all this," Murphy says as he pulls into the parking lot of a closed down carryout.

"Why is this happening now?" I ask.

"AFK almost killed Paul. He successfully killed Paul's lawyer and his right hand man. To the Cabal, that equals open season. To the Alphas, that has to mean re-establishing strength. Think about it, almost every top ranking Alpha member was murdered by AFK or was incarcerated and gave up information about the Alpha case," Parker says as he picks up his phone to call for support.

"My kids are at that hospital," I say as I witness Paul running down the street and looking back. I look back at the person chasing Paul and notice Darrin with a gun in hand, running down an alley, possibly trying to cut Paul off. The windows to the SUV are tinted; I'm sure they never saw me in the car.

When I glance back towards Paul, I notice that he is attempting to break into Hakeem's church, New Hope Greater Love. Murphy and Parker are distracted trying to call for help and support as the sound of helicopters can be heard in the sky above. I open the car door and run to the church behind Paul. Maybe I can finish what I started. Maybe I can save his life. Maybe I can stop Darrin from making a huge mistake. No matter what, he's not going to destroy the church that my grandmother helped build.

As I open the door and run out of the SUV towards the church, as I hear Murphy yell for me to stay. Murphy and Parker yell for me to come back, but I keep running. I hear shots ring out towards their SUV, but don't look back because I need to get inside the church.

The feeling of fear is nonexistence during this time, but anger and rage towards Paul consumes me, along with my concern for and frustration about Darrin. I hear several gunshots and yelling around me. The city sounds like it is on fire. Several homes and corner stores are burning around me as I continue to head towards the church.

Chapter 20

As I open the broken glass door and enter the vestibule area of the church, I glance over at the announcement board, the worship hall doors, the bathrooms and the steps. I peek into the children's church classroom and the little chapel, and hear nothing. The darkness of the night floods the church building. The only visible light is from the set fires in the community, lights from the police cars, EMTs, fire trucks, and the helicopter spotlights. I can see the green light from the exit sign in the back of the worship hall.

There is an unsteady silence in the church building, along with a strange chill in the air. The silence in the church is maddening because of the sounds normally heard in this building. On any given day you would hear the musicians, members of the choir, the step team, the dancers practicing or ministering or hear participants in the addictions or grief and loss groups in deep conversation. Today, nothing.

"So we're going to do round 2 in the church?" Bell asks in my ear, disturbing the silence that has become very unsettling. Even with all of the noise and rage outside, the four walls of this church are silent, untouched, sovereign.

"Don't go into the sanctuary," Bell says as I open the door to the almost completely dark chapel. I can't see much of anything except for the eerie glow from the exit sign.

"You shouldn't be here," Paul says. It sounds like his voice is near the front of the church.

"I could say the same thing," I respond as I hear what sounds like something heavy hit the wall beside me. Did he just throw something at me?

"I'm done fighting you. I'm done with all of this. I'm done. I can't do this no more. AFK just killed my best friend," Paul says and I hear another loud thud. Maybe he kicked or punched something, I'm unable to tell.

"The lawyer?" I ask as I hear a louder thud.

"No, my friend Roland. He lost everything. His wife, his kids. He had his loyalty to me. And because of your aunt, everything is gone. Honestly, I didn't even want to hurt y'all. I just wanted your aunt's head."

"I have nothing to do with her," I explain and then jump as something else hits the wall behind me with extreme force.

"Your aunt called out NAFA and Sergeant Bell. Bell gathered a group of my Alphas and took over the streets of Baltimore, ignoring all the deals I had in place. Then Bell took a deal with the district attorney and had my own people snitching on me. As a result I looked weak. Not only that, the Action Figure Killer is running around killing anybody closely related to me. Again, making me look weak."

"You *are* weak," A young voice says as a gunshot rings out. The flash came from near where I was standing and hit something in the front of the church. I quickly realize the voice is Darrin's.

"Who said that?" Paul asks as he returns gun fire, striking the wall behind me. I quickly take cover behind a pew. The feeling of fear begins to overtake me. This has now turned into a life or death situation, and I'm just now fully appreciating the seriousness of following Paul into a dark and empty church.

"You know how many of my friends you killed? You burned my house down! You sent my sister to the hospital! You killed Jamar!" Darrin says as he fires off two more shots. All that can be seen is the flash, as Paul returns fire in that direction.

"Is this one of your kids, Tiffy?" Paul asks as my heart begins beating faster and faster. I feel trapped.

"What, you called your son for backup because I beat your ass a few minutes ago?" Paul continues as several glass windows to the church shatter. Moments later fire fills the chapel and the pews, musical instruments, chairs and communion tables are visible, thanks to the flickering flames.

The noise from outside comes flooding in, along with the police lights.

"You see this, Tiffy? This is what power and fear gets you. A war," Paul says as I look around for Darrin.

"I don't need to go to the police for a deal because I don't plan on living in this city alive, but I will leave a mark in the history books," Paul says as he stands up and begins walking near the choir loft behind the pulpit area.

"Where is that kid of yours? I heard he is a member of the Cabal. I want to see what he's really about," Paul says as I see Darrin's head pop up in a pew on my right side, slightly in front of me. He pulls the trigger and the gun shoots multiple shots until there is a clicking sound. Paul fires a revolver in Darrin's direction and I hear him scream and fall to the floor.

"Darrin!" I scream as Paul turns the gun in my direction. We both begin to cough and choke from the fire. I hear my son cry out in pain.

"Leave him, he's mine," Paul says in a forceful tone before coughing excessively.

Something bounces near the front of the church and then suddenly there's an explosion that destroys the chairs and instruments in the pulpit area.

I hear several gunshots as Paul takes cover behind the wooden piano. As Darrin moans in pain, I hear several items roll on the floor, followed by loud explosions and flashes. Smoke from the fire consumes the inside of the church, along with white smoke from one of the explosions. My eyes and skin begin to burn as gas fills the church. All the cuts and bruises on my face, arms and legs are on fire as gas spreads throughout the sanctuary. My nose begins to run in a steady stream, and I can barely see as I hear footsteps down the center of the church, followed by the racking of a shotgun.

"Darrin, run out the back door!" I scream to my son.

"He stays here with me," Paul says as a loud shotgun blast follows, hitting the wooden piano. The piano responds to the blast with an off key sound, as if someone mashed on several keys at once. I hear scurrying in the pulpit area as I try to get near the rear of the church. I notice the man in riot gear that was at Vernon Shaw's office, walking in the center of the church.

"Who the hell is that?" Darrin asks as he tries to run to the back door.

"That's AFK," I answer as the person glances back at Darrin and me making our way to the rear of the church. On the floor, I notice several green Army men toys.

Paul fires a shot, hitting the rear of the church near me as I duck back behind the rear pew, making eye contact with Darrin. My son is holding his left arm as if in pain, as we hear AFK rack the shotgun again.

"That's not the same guy that burned our house down," Darrin says to me as another shotgun blast is heard and one of the chairs in the pulpit is hit. Paul stands up to shoot AFK, but there is a click, signaling he is out of ammunition. He then runs behind the wooden pulpit stand, the same one that Pastor Avery and Hakeem have preached behind several times, as AFK fires another shot in his direction.

Paul then charges towards AFK as the man in riot gear places his left arm between Paul's legs and his right arm behind his neck, scooping Paul off the floor, then slamming him back down. Barely able to breathe, I open the double doors in the rear of the church as the fire continues to spread.

Paul and AFK continue to fight. AFK rubs Paul's head on the floor of the church and hits him with forearms to the back of the head. AFK attempts to choke Paul, until Paul retrieves a knife from his pocket and stabs AFK in the thigh. Paul crawls away from AFK until the man in riot gear grabs his ankle and twists it.

Picking up a shard of glass laying on the floor, Paul stabs AFK's right arm and begins running towards the open double doors until he is tackled in the vestibule by AFK. The two trade punches until the riot gear helmet is knocked off revealing that AFK has a ski mask on underneath that only displays his eyes and his nasal bridge.

Looking out the broken glass door at the front of the church, I see the flashing lights of several police cars, EMTs and firefighters. I turn my attention back towards my son who is bleeding profusely. I grab him and hold him close. I think about all the times he fell and hurt himself as a child. The first time I saw him fall and bleed. The first time he cried in the hospital. The first time he went to school. The look on his face when I told him his sister, Kenya, died in a car accident. I'm not losing my son. I find the wound the blood is pouring from, and rip off a part of my black dress, near my thighs to make a tourniquet on his forearm.

Paul meets AFK with a series of punches as the two are now on their feet. AFK pulls out a large military style knife and slashes at Paul, cutting him several times until Paul grabs AFK's arm and slings him into the glass door. Paul then takes another shard of glass and stabs AFK in the back, near his spine.

Grabbing a baton from out of one of his pockets, AFK is slow to turn around. Paul connects a right hook to AFK's jaw, knocking him down. When AFK falls, the baton rolls near Paul's foot, and he glances at me before he picks it up.

"I really wish you would have gotten that salad," Paul says before hitting AFK repeatedly across the back, neck and head with it. Paul attempts to choke AFK with the baton around his neck as AFK runs backwards with Paul on his back, crushing him against the announcement board. The impact frees AFK from the hold, as he and Paul hit the ground. The two lay on the ground for a moment as the sound of the ceiling crashing to the floor in the sanctuary can be heard from the vestibule.

Coughing uncontrollably, AFK yanks off his mask revealing his identity to be Alex Tillman. He attempts to catch his breath before looking at Darrin and me, then back to Paul, who is attempting to regain his composure.

AFK turns completely around, runs with his head down, and arms wrapped around Paul's waist, ramming him into the wall with all of his might. Paul's back hits the announcement bulletin, causing the wooden frame to break apart and fall to the floor, along with a gray handgun that falls out of one of AFK's pockets. AFK and Paul begin to trade punches. Darrin and I escape out the front door as the police and members of the community fight the rioting gang members across the street in front of the residential homes.

I turn back around and notice AFK placing a zip tie handcuff around Paul's neck as Paul has a handgun trained in my direction. Darrin rushes in front of me to shield me from the gunshot. Paul's eyes grow large and he drops the gun, falls to his knees and grabs for the zip tie. AFK picks Paul up over his head, hoisting him as high as he can, and throws Paul down the cement steps in the front of the church. AFK broods over having engaged in such a lengthy altercation with Paul and then notices Paul has stopped moving. He shrugs before turning his attention to the fighting in the community.

AFK then glares towards my son and me, then he walks back into the church, gathers his mask and riot helmet and reapplies them. We make eye contact one last time before he walks down the steps, places multiple plastic bags on Paul's head, positions several green Army men nearby, and walks away.

"Nobody saw him?" Darrin asks as we walk down the stairs of the church that have begun to fall apart.

I look at my son, then back at the church that I grew up in. A place that was a safe haven for me as a child. A safe haven because my mother would bring me here, and my uncle Larry or my grandmother Florence would take me to their house after service. We had family dinners, we had discussions, we had a normal life on Sundays. Now my house is gone and so is this church.

I see the look on Darrin's face, as he waits for an answer. The shooting has quieted, the police have gathered rioters and gang members, Alphas and Cabal alike. EMTs finally arrive shortly afterwards to take my son to the same emergency room my youngest daughter was pronounced dead in close to four years ago. I still have no words. I do know that I saved my son's life tonight by applying a tourniquet.

Chapter 21

A few weeks after the day and night from hell, the community starts to ask questions about where to go next. Erica Little has made relentless requests to purchase all homes, damaged or not, at top dollar. The events of that night turn into a political agenda.

The surviving Alpha and Cabal members grow quiet. The crime rate drops dramatically. My daughter, Trinity returns home from the burn unit, and Darrin survives his gunshot wound. The doctor says the bullet went in and out cleanly, and if I hadn't made the tourniquet, my son would have bled out and died. I guess nursing school has its benefits, even though after I graduated with a bachelor's degree in social work, I became a restauranteur and bank owner.

Inside of the Legacy of Florence restaurant, Detective Murphy and Agent Parker are sitting at a booth across from Hakeem and me. It is early in the day, the breakfast crowd is packed tight and enjoying themselves. The televisions above the bar relay stories about sports and the events that led to what is now touted as "The Ridgely

Square Incident." Any mention of the "Incident" leads to thousands of social media clicks and newspapers being sold.

"The Action Figure Killer case is now closed," Detective Murphy says as he chews on his sandwich.

"Oh, you got him?" I ask, with concern for Alex Tillman. I didn't hear anything about it on the news.

"No, he was murdered by Paul Douglass at Vernon Shaw's law office," Detective Murphy answers as Agent Parker starts looking through his phone.

"What are you talking about? The only person killed at the law office that night was Roland Wise. He was the copycat AFK," I respond. Murphy has a large smile on his face.

"The City of Baltimore has refused to pay for any more services from the FBI relative to the Alpha sex trafficking case, or AFK. That being said, our new police commissioner will make an announcement soon that Roland Wise was the Action Figure Killer, and was murdered by the copycat AFK," Murphy states.

"Who would be the copycat AFK?" Hakeem asks, upset by the politics involved with this change of events.

"Paul Douglass," Murphy answers quickly, "after attempting to burn down your home, destroy your restaurant, bank and kill everyone you're related to and love. Paul Douglass went to set the church on fire and then commit suicide, making himself a religious martyr for the Alphas."

"You think that's going to fly? What happens when the real AFK strikes again?" I ask.

"We're detectives not brain surgeons," Murphy answers. "We could be completely wrong, and nobody would bat an eye. In this line of work the truth is not what you know but what you can prove."

"Were you able to identify who Action Figure Killer is?" Agent Parker asks and I shake my head no. I hear Bell's voice compliment me for not saying anything.

"You came in close contact with this guy, or gal twice and you can't tell me who they are?" Murphy asks as he continues to eat his sandwich.

"He was strong and white. That's all I know. Hell, he could be you, Detective Murphy," I say. He chuckles.

"You saw who he was, didn't you?" Detective Murphy asks as he lowers his head closer to the table.

"I don't know who he was," I return.

"Let's say you did, would you promise to talk to me first before telling the news media or anything like that?" Murphy asks.

"Why?" Hakeem asks. "You got what you wanted. An open and shut case, with a secret that everyone at this table will have to take to the grave because the city doesn't want to invest more into the case to stop a serial killer."

"There's tons of serial killers that the city and the state refuse to invest in. There's a group of white supremacists, called the Right Hand of God, that come to the city to go hunting for black men every month. They ride in their pickup trucks to urban areas during the daytime and shoot one black man, taking a trophy, like shoes, a chain, a watch, or a piece of hair. The governor stopped that investigation, and made me destroy all evidence related to it," Murphy reports.

"What?" Hakeem and I say at the same time.

"That's one of the reasons why I was a beat cop for years. I discovered that several years ago. When I was finally promoted to detective, that case stayed on my mind and I kept looking into it. That's not important. What is important is that you let me know if you see the real AFK murdering people again," Murphy reiterates.

"Why is it so important?" I ask.

"Let's say you do know who he is. You decide to tell the wrong or right officer, or investigator. That raises a lot of questions related to the job he used to work, and a lot of the bad people he put away can win an appeal and come back on the street," Murphy explains and we both nod in agreement.

"So we're going to just cover this up?" I ask. Murphy says yes and Parker continues to play on his phone.

"So what's next for you, Agent Parker?" Hakeem asks. The special agent looks in our direction.

"I have to go down to Georgia to investigate a person smuggling drugs and women from country to country. They're in some way tied to a cartel. Nothing major," Agent Parker says looking back at his phone.

"Well gentlemen, I wish you the best. You're always welcome to come here," I state as I leave the table with Hakeem, Murphy, and Parker and head to my office in the back.

As I open the door and walk into the office I notice my light was left on. Something I never do. I close the door behind me and find Alex Tillman sitting in my chair with a gun pointing towards me and a green Army man toy sitting upright on the desk.

"Scream and I'll kill you," he says as I place my hands in the air, partially pissing myself. "Grab a chair, I'd like to chat."

I walk over to one of the chairs in front of my desk and sit down as I stare at the barrel of the gun pointed at me. It is a blue steel revolver.

"I'm going to ask you a few questions. The moment you lie, I'm going to kill you. Understood?" he asks and I nod yes. "Are you now or were you ever affiliated with the Alphas?" Alex Tillman asks me, and I say no.

"Are you smuggling money for the Alphas or any of their operations?" Alex asks as I take a deep breath. I hear my grandmother's voice begging me to be honest.

"I didn't originally. I started this company with the inheritance and insurance money I received from my grandmother. When Jamar, Claire, Hakeem, and a few others started the 10th Bank, I thought everything was legit. I learned moments before you burst into Vernon Shaw's law office, that someone was washing money through my bank without my knowledge," I answer.

"Have you ever knowingly taken illegal money?" Alex asks, gripping the gun and pointing it towards me.

"The night you killed Marshawn Bell. He kidnapped me from my home. Made me give his mother medication in an IV drip until we reached the treatment center in Newport News, Virginia. When we arrived there he told me he had several millions in gift cards for me. It was for my pain and suffering," I answer.

"Did you spend it?"

"Not a dime."

"Why?" Alex asks with his pointer finger tapping the barrel of the revolver.

"I didn't feel it was right. But then again, if my kids ever needed it, it felt good to know it was there. But I would have only touched it as a last resort," I say as sadness begins to fall upon me. Alex stops pointing the gun at me and places it in his pocket.

"It's behind the picture on the wall, next to me. The picture with you and your family. It's in a safe with the combination 1-2-34," he says. To my surprise, he's completely accurate.

"Every gift card, with every single cent, is still in that safe, still in the bag, you got into my car with. Impressive," Alex says, looking around the office at multiple pictures. He relaxes his posture in the chair as he looks at me.

"I'm not going to kill you, Ms. Gibbons, but I did want to tell you why I did what I did. You're one of the few people that know that I'm the real AFK."

"You don't have to do that," I mention, looking back at the office door in fear.

"I do. My son, John. He loved me. I was his hero. I was a crappy husband, putting my job as a police officer first all the time. But I was a great father. I got to keep him after the divorce. My son used to collect these Army men toys. I would buy them from the Rite Aid pharmacy when he was little. When he graduated high school he and his friends went to Tennessee on a hiking trip," Alex says as I wonder where this conversation is heading. If anyone walks into this office, he will surely kill them and me.

"Anna Cartwright was the State's Attorney in Tennessee at the time. She was caught up in a scandal for receiving financial kickbacks from prisons for incarcerations. She was removed from office, and several cases she presided over were flipped. Freeing several bad people. One of those bad people was the psychotic man that killed my son. He didn't kill my son because I was a police officer, or because my son was in a gang. He killed him because he wanted to know if he still 'had it.' A convicted felon with four life sentences without the option of parole, freed to kill my son."

"I'm so sorry to hear that," I state.

"Anna came here to Maryland, and got a night show. She then started working for Nubian Media. My son was still dead, so I killed the man who killed my son, leaving a toy that I found in his room. Nobody thought to look for me or fingerprint the toy. I was ashamed that I got away with that crime, to be honest."

"Why are you telling me all of this?" I ask as Alex shakes his head.

"I need to tell somebody," Alex answers. "When I moved up through the ranks at the police department, there were two guys that felt like sons to me: Edward Carter and Marshawn Bell. I was heartbroken the day Edward Carter was murdered. I loved him like I loved John. He was a good guy, with a great heart. I was the person that returned fire and killed the two gang members that killed him. Nobody asked how I was doing. They talked about Kennard Lyles-Bey and Tyrone Clinton. Nobody cared about my safety or any of my other officers."

"I'm so sorry that people were insensitive," I state as Alex dismisses my statement.

"My heart melted that day in court when I learned that Marshawn Bell paid the Alphas to murder Edward Carter. I felt that it was my responsibility to put him down. I allowed him to get away with questionable behavior for too long, without punishment. I wanted to stay in prison or get a lethal injection. Instead, I was given the option to work with the FBI on the Alpha case. I gave them my expertise, but I cleaned up Marshawn Bell's mess in the process. Getting rid of every Alpha member I could get my hands on."

"What about the former police chief and the former city councilman?" I ask, in shock by his confession.

"The city councilman used to pay for the sexual services of underaged girls, provided by the Alphas. The former police chief tipped off so many people that were under investigation. Same with the former State's Attorney. Instead of turning evidence over related to Marshawn Bell, NAFA or the Alphas, she held on to it with the goal of advancing her career. I corrected the wrongs that Marshawn Bell left. It wasn't pretty, but it needed to be done," Alex says before standing up and placing a gym bag on the table. He unzipped it, to display several $50 and $100 bills bound together.

"I went inside of Paul Douglass's home and found this stash in one of his closets. There was a lot more stashed in shoe boxes, trash cans and cereal boxes. I figured you could use this for your wedding. I truly wish you the best. Your grandmother and Pastor Avery were great people. I really think this community will be in great hands with you and Hakeem," Alex says, walking to my side. The hairs on my neck begin to rise as he stands over me.

"Can I hold your phone?" he asks as I concede and hand it to him. "During the start of the investigation when I met with you, along with Detective Murphy and Agent Parker, I placed my phone number in your phone. I also turned on a location share on your phone, so that I could monitor your movements."

Alex poked around on my phone before handing it back to me, and then walked to the door.

"Where are you headed now?" I ask as Alex stops for a brief moment and turns towards me.

"I'm in the wind. Don't look for me." Alex says before walking out of the office and out of my restaurant.

Chapter 22

Later that evening, I sit inside the hospital room with my mother, who is receiving palliative care because of her organ failure. It is the night of the election. Hakeem is with Mya Rodriguez's camp at my restaurant. They have high hopes of celebrating a victory together. Desha, RJ and Trinity are with Hakeem at the restaurant. Darrin is in the room with me, sleeping in the corner, rested against the wall. Since the "Ridgely Square Incident," Darrin has refused to leave my side, except for when he is in school. Which is pretty easy, seeing that we have all been staying at Hakeem's house until our home reconstruction is finished.

I glance at my mother, who looks like a shell of her former self, as several thoughts run through my mind. I'm not sad. I think I need closure. But what closure do I need? My mother wasn't a mother to me. She allowed my father to rape and abuse me growing up. She was in denial about all of the events that took place.

I'm not sure if I'm harboring anger towards my mother or not. Is it worth it? Look at her. Weak. Unaware of what's going on. Not able to feed herself, or do for herself. I was unable to do for myself when my dad abused me, but she didn't care. Why am I here caring? Am I the bigger person? Should I have to be? I'm not broken. I took the power back that my father took from me. The day I pulled the trigger and took his life was the first day that his shadow vanished from over me.

But my mother. She was never my mother. She was never my protector. She was never my role model. I remember when I was young, I was in church, Sunday School. We had to talk in front of the church about something, I don't remember what exactly. I drew a comic, I used to be a great artist. I was accepted into this nationally recognized art school. Anyway, I drew this comic strip. It had my mother watching soap operas, my dad shirtless smoking a cigarette, and me doing homework. People in the church laughed and thought it was entertaining. Not my mother. She told my father, Daryl "Cube" Gibbons. He decided to disconnect the cable box and beat me with the coax cable. I never drew again and was expelled from the art school.

As I look at my mother lying in the Hill-Rom bed, I realize I'm not angry at her anymore. I don't feel bad for her either. It was best that things ended this way. My mother was a constant reminder of all that I endured with my father. "I have grown from being a victim to a homeowner, a mother, a college graduate, an entrepreneur and soon to be a wife. Even with those accomplishments, you would have never celebrated me. You would have found ways to tear me down. I became successful in spite of you." I say with confidence.

I heard a gospel song with lyrics that say, "The battle is not yours, it's the Lord's." I guess He saw to it that I won. Jamar used to say, "You can't live in the Promised Land unless you kill the natives that are currently living there. You know, the giants that lived in the Promised Land. You were one of my biggest giants and now look at you, lying on your back and looking up at me."

"Are you sure this is healthy?" Bell asks.

"I just want to point out that she can go any minute now. It's best to get your final goodbye in now. The last thing we need is another figment of a person's voice here taking up more headspace and living rent free," Bell continues as I see my mother's hands resting at her sides.

"When are you going to tell Hakeem about his adopted sister and what she's done?" Bell asks as I answer, "We won't."

To be continued in *The Union.*

About the Author

Dr. Kyle Berkley is a husband and father from Baltimore, Maryland. After graduating from Fredrick Douglass High School in Baltimore City, Kyle attended Coppin State College with a major in history. During that time Kyle produced and wrote songs for hip hop, R&B, country, and gospel music artists. Kyle would later continue his education at Sojourner Douglass College and Morgan State University, where he earned his Bachelor's and Master's degrees in Social Work. Kyle also earned a Master's degree in Philosophy and a Ph.D. in Human and Social Services from Walden University. In 2012, Kyle and his wife, Rebecca, created a nonprofit organization called the 4 Us Initiative that provides safe housing for victims of domestic violence, homeless families, and preventive care for adolescents.

In 2014, Kyle was elected as a representative to the Baltimore City State Central Committee. Along with serving on the State Central Committee, Kyle has provided mental health therapy, grief counseling, and case management at Baltimore City shelters, hospitals, medical centers, transitional houses, outpatient medical, crisis response teams, The American Red Cross, and substance abuse treatment centers.

Kyle Berkley released his first novel in 2018 entitled *The Wake*. *The Void* is his second novel. In his free time, Kyle can be found cooking, playing video games with his 3 daughters, enjoying vacation trips with his wife, reading, and watching movies. Kyle is a huge history buff and comic book collector. Kyle also enjoys fishing, playing sports, weight lifting, engaging in casual debates on various subjects, praying, helping people in need, and spending time with his family.

A Letter from the Author

Take a deep breath, we made it to the end of The Legacy! We learned about the Action Figure Killer, we gained more insight into the Alphas and how they operate. It was great to give a little insight into how the Baltimore City Police viewed NAFA. Random question, if you place AFK and Marshawn Bell side-by-side, who do you think was worse? Think about that for a little bit.

I'm excited about the next two installments in this series, *The Union and The Transition,* and where Tiffany goes now that she is free from the shadow of her parents. Also, where does Tiffany go now that she has been stripped away from so many things that tied her to her grandmother? Where does Hakeem go from here? What role does Hakeem's sister play in everything? Was Erica Little right? Did Titan Industries win in the long run? What role will Mya play going forward? We're going to figure this out in *The Union.*

BOOKS BY THIS AUTHOR

visit www.kylesberkley.com

www.amazon.com/stores/Kyle-S.-Berkley/author/B07FK2YRT6

About the Author

Dr. Kyle Berkley is a husband and father from Baltimore, Maryland. After graduating from Fredrick Douglass High School in Baltimore City, Kyle attended Coppin State College with a major in history. During that time Kyle produced and wrote songs for hip hop, R&B, country, and gospel music artists. Kyle would later continue his education at Sojourner Douglass College and Morgan State University, where he earned his Bachelor's and Master's degrees in Social Work. Kyle also earned a Master's degree in Philosophy and a Ph.D. in Human and Social Services from Walden University. In 2012, Kyle and his wife, Rebecca, created a nonprofit organization called the 4 Us Initiative that provides safe housing for victims of domestic violence, homeless families, and preventive care for adolescents.

In 2014, Kyle was elected as a representative to the Baltimore City State Central Committee. Along with serving on the State Central Committee, Kyle has provided mental health therapy, grief counseling, and case management at Baltimore City shelters, hospitals, medical centers, transitional houses, outpatient medical, crisis response teams, The American Red Cross, and substance abuse treatment centers.

Kyle Berkley released his first novel in 2018 entitled *The Wake*. *The Void* was his second novel, and the first book in the Tiffany Gibbons Saga. In his free time, Kyle can be found cooking, playing video games with his 3 daughters, enjoying vacation trips with his wife, reading, and watching movies. Kyle is a huge history buff and comic book collector. Kyle also enjoys fishing, playing sports, weight lifting, engaging in casual debates on various subjects, praying, helping people in need, and spending time with his family.